THE SWEET-SCENTED NAME

THE
SWEET-SCENTED NAME

AND OTHER FAIRY TALES, FABLES
AND STORIES

BY

FEDOR SOLOGUB
(Fedor Kuzmich Teternikov)

EDITED BY

STEPHEN GRAHAM

Short Story Index Reprint Series

BOOKS FOR LIBRARIES PRESS
FREEPORT, NEW YORK

First Published 1915
Reprinted 1972

INTERNATIONAL STANDARD BOOK NUMBER:
0-8369-4124-1

LIBRARY OF CONGRESS CATALOG CARD NUMBER:
73-37565

PRINTED IN THE UNITED STATES OF AMERICA
BY
NEW WORLD BOOK MANUFACTURING CO., INC.
HALLANDALE, FLORIDA 33009

CONTENTS

THE SWEET-SCENTED NAME

INTRODUCTION

FEDOR SOLOGUB is one of the cleverest of contemporary Russian tale-writers and poets. He ranks with Tchekhof and Kuprin and Remizof, though he has very little in common with these writers. He is not a realist; he does not love to comment on life as Tchekhof did, nor to flood his pages with delicious details as does Kuprin; he has nothing of either the melancholy or the energy of Gorky. He is more modern than these; he scents new thoughts, and endeavours to find a new medium of style and language to present them to his age. His genius lies in the power he has to suggest atmosphere. He can cast the reader into a spell and then say magical sentences in his ears—it may be a sweet spell as in " Turandina " or a terrible one as in " The Herald of the Beast," but the reader is infallibly beguiled out of the everyday atmosphere into the mirage or phantasy or trance which the author, who is a sort of Prospero, wishes.

Apart from this magic, Sologub possesses and exhibits a pleasant sense of humour. His witty fables, of which only a few are interspersed in these pages, are famous in Russia. In politics he is a Liberal, and is capable of biting satire. Like Biely and Andreef and Kuprin, and many another Russian writer, he was infected by despair after the Russo-Japanese war and the bloody revolutionary era. The literature of 1906, 1907, 1908 was marked by hysteria, and several of Sologub's tales of that time are incoherent through grief. But as the years go on he is quickly convalescent. As Russia righted herself he recovered, and in the time before the great war of 1914 he is found in halcyon mood. One would hardly dream that public events and the political well-being of his nation could affect the author of such stories as these, and yet there is always the reflection of the Russia of the hour in the story of the hour. Such respon-

INTRODUCTION

siveness to national moods is characteristic of national life.

Sologub's works comprise two novels, *The Little Demon* and *Drops of Blood,* a volume of poems, some essays, and about a dozen volumes of short tales. This volume, which my wife and I have selected and translated, is offered as a foretaste of some very remarkable work.

Russia is the land of such short tales. Long novels are exceptional and not very popular. Nearly all Russian writers of note to-day are either poets or essayists or short-story writers. Tchekhof, who wrote some twenty volumes of little tales, really made the short story popular. " I have made a way for this sort of writing," he is reported to have said to Kuprin. " After me it will be easy for others to go on writing such tales." The prophecy has been fulfilled. More than eighty per cent of the fiction published since his death has been collections of little stories.

Fedor Sologub is one of the cleverest of these writers of tales. He has reduced the short story to a minimum, and some of his cleverest efforts do not exceed half a page

in length. Many are little more than epi-
grams, and give one the idea that they were
probably written at the oddest moments,
between courses at dinner, whilst waiting
for an answer to a riddle, in bed, in cabs.
The author is notoriously eccentric in life.

Most of these stories were originally published in Russian newspapers, and only after
some time collected into volumes. The
Russian newspapers give the hospitality of
their columns to many short stories and
sketches. Long-winded serials are almost
unknown in the press, and indeed the public
demands a type of literature much higher
than that which commonly adorns the
columns of our British daily papers. The
feuilleton of the Russian newspaper is generally either a quarter-page article written by
one of the brilliant publicists of the day, such
as Rozanof or Merezhkovsky, or a short
tale by Sologub or Kuprin or Gorky, or
one or other of the great Russian tale-writers.
A great number of Sologub's stories have, for
instance, appeared in the *Retch*. Of those
given in the present volume, " Lohengrin,"
" Who art Thou ? " and " The Hungry

INTRODUCTION

Gleam " appeared in the *Retch*; " She who wore a Crown " in the *Russian Word*; " Turandina " in the *Voice of the Earth*; " The Kiss of the Unborn " in the *Morning of Russia*; " The River Mairure " in *Our Life*; " The Crimson Ribbon " in the *New Word*— all daily newspapers of Russia. All the stories were written within the last ten years. Of these translations " Wings " and " The Sweet-scented Name " appeared in *Country Life,* and that journal retains the right to reproduce them in a volume of Russian fairy-tales and fables if it so desires.

STEPHEN GRAHAM.

Wings

A PEASANT girl was feeding geese, and she wept. The farmer's daughter came by and asked, " What are you blubbering about ? "

" I haven't got any wings," cried the peasant girl. " Oh, I wish I could grow some wings."

" You stupid ! " said the farmer's daughter. " Of course you haven't got wings. What do you want wings for ? "

" I want to fly up into the sky and sing my little songs there," answered the little peasant girl.

Then the farmer's daughter was angry, and said again, " You stupid ! How can you ever expect to grow wings ? Your father's only a farm-labourer. They might grow on me, but not on you."

When the farmer's daughter had said that, she went away to the well, sprinkled some water on her shoulders, and stood out among the vegetables in the garden, waiting

1 B

for her wings to sprout. She really believed the sun would bring them out quite soon.

But in a little while a merchant's daughter came along the road and called out to the girl who was trying to grow wings in the garden, " What are you doing standing out there, red face ? "

" I am growing wings," said the farmer's daughter. " I want to fly."

Then the merchant's daughter laughed loudly, and cried out, " You stupid farm-girl ; if you had wings they would only be a weight on your back."

The merchant's daughter thought she knew who was most likely to grow wings. And when she went back to the town where she lived she bought some olive - oil and rubbed it on her shoulders, and went out into the garden and waited for her wings to grow.

By and by a young lady of the Court came along and said to her, " What are you doing out there, my child ? "

When the tradesman's daughter said that she was growing wings, the young lady's face flushed and she looked quite vexed. " That's not for you to do," she said. " It is only real ladies who can grow wings."

And she went on home, and when she got

indoors she filled a tub with milk and bathed herself in it, and then went into her garden and stood in the sun and waited for her wings to come out.

Presently a princess passed by the garden, and when she saw the young lady standing there she sent a servant to inquire what she was doing. The servant came back and told her that as the young lady had wanted to be able to fly she had bathed herself in milk and was waiting for her wings to grow.

The princess laughed scornfully and exclaimed, " What a foolish girl ! She's giving herself trouble for nothing. No one who is not a princess can ever grow wings."

The princess turned the matter over in her mind, and when she arrived at her father's palace she went into her chamber, anointed herself with sweet-smelling perfumes, and then went down into the palace garden to wait for her wings to come.

Very soon all the young girls in the country round about went out into their gardens and stood among the vegetables so that they might get wings.

The Fairy of the Wings heard about this strange happening and she flew down to earth, and, looking at the waiting girls, she said, " If I give you all wings and let you all go flying in the sky, who will want to stay at home to cook the porridge and look after the children ? I had better only give wings to one of you, namely to her who wanted them first of all."

So wings grew from the little peasant girl's shoulders, and she was able to fly up into the sky and sing.

The Sweet-Scented Name

A LITTLE peasant girl lay ill in her bed. And in heaven God called an angel to His side and bade her go down to earth and dance before the little girl and amuse her. But the angel thought it unbecoming to her dignity to dance before the people of the earth.

And God knew the proud thoughts of the angel and ordained a punishment for her. She was born into the world of men and became a little child there—a princess in a royal house—and she forgot all that she had known of heaven and her former life, forgot even her own name.

Now the angel had been called by a name of purity and fragrance, and the people of the earth know no such names as these. So when she became an earthly princess she had only a human name, and was called the Princess Margaret.

When the little princess grew up she often felt as if she wanted to remember something she had once known, but she could not think what it might be, and she became unhappy because she could not remember.

One day she asked her father :

" How is it we cannot hear the sunshine ? "

The king smiled at the question, but he could not answer it, and the little princess looked very grieved.

Another day she said to her mother :

" The roses smell very sweet ; how is it I cannot see their scent ? " And when her mother laughed at the strange question the princess felt sadder than ever.

Some time afterwards she came to her nurse and said :

" How is it that names are not sweet-scented ? "

The old nurse laughed at her, and again the princess was grieved that no one could answer any of her questions. Then a rumour went about the land that the king's daughter was different from other people, and that her mind was weak. And everybody tried to think of some means to cure her and make her well.

She was a quiet and melancholy child, and was always asking strange and unusual questions. She was thin and pale, and no one thought her beautiful. But she grew older, and at last the time came for her to marry. Many young princes came to her father's court to woo her, but when she began to talk to them no one wanted to have her as a wife. At last a prince named Maximilian arrived, and when the princess saw him she said to him :

"With us human beings everything seems quite separate from other things—I can only *hear* words, I cannot smell them ; and though I can see flowers and smell their scent, yet I cannot hear them. It makes life dull and uninteresting, don't you think ?"

"What would make life more beautiful for you ?" said Maximilian.

The princess was silent for some time, but at last she said, " I should so much like to have a sweet-smelling name."

"Yes, fair princess," said he, " the name Margaret is not nearly good enough for you. You ought to have a name of sweet fragrance, but there are no such names known upon the earth." Then the poor little princess wept sad tears, and Maximilian felt very sorry for her, and he loved her more than any one else in the whole world. He tried to comfort her by saying, " Do not weep, dear princess. I will try and find out if

7

there are such names, and come and tell you of them."

The princess smiled through her tears and said, " If you can find for me a name which gives forth a sweet odour when it is spoken, then I will kiss your stirrup-leather." And she blushed as she said this, for she was a princess and very proud.

Hearing this, Maximilian grew bolder and said, " And will you then be my wife ? " And the princess answered that she would.

So Maximilian departed to search throughout all the world until he found a name which would give forth a sweet fragrance and perfume the air when it was spoken. He travelled into far lands and made inquiries of rich and poor, learned and ignorant; but everybody laughed at his quest, and told him he had set out upon a foolish errand. At last, after long journeying, he came again to the town where the princess dwelt. Just outside the town was a peasant's cottage, and at the door stood an old white-haired man. As soon as Maximilian saw him he thought in his heart " the old man will know," and he went up to him and told him of his quest, and how he was in search of a sweet-smelling name.

The old man looked up gladly and

answered at once, " Yes, yes ; there is such a name—a holy and spiritual name it is. I myself do not know this name, but my little grandchild has heard it."

So Maximilian went with the old man into the poor cottage, and there he saw a little peasant girl lying ill in her bed. The old man went up to her and said, " Doonia, here is a gentleman who wants to know the holy name you told me of ; can you remember it and tell him ? "

The little girl looked joyfully at Maximilian and smiled sweetly at him, but she could not remember the wonderful name. She told the prince that in a dream an angel had come to her and danced before her, and as she watched the angel she saw that his garment was of many colours, like a soft rainbow. Then the angel had talked to her, and had told her that soon another angel would come and visit her and would dance before her in still more beautiful colours than those she had seen. He told her the angel's name, and as she heard the name she smelt a delicious fragrance, and all the air was filled with a sweet scent. " But now," said the child, " I cannot remember that wonderful name, though it still makes me happy to think about it.

THE SWEET-SCENTED NAME

If only I could remember it and say it myself I think I should be quite well again. But the beautiful angel will soon come, and then I shall remember the name."

Maximilian went away to the palace and told the princess all that had befallen him, and she came with him to the cottage to visit the sick girl. As soon as she saw the child she was filled with pity for her, and sat down by her side and petted her, and tried to think of something that would amuse her and make her forget her pain.

By and by she got up and began to dance before the sick child, clapping her hands together, and singing. And as the little girl watched the princess she saw all kinds of lovely colours and heard many beautiful sounds. She felt very happy, and she laughed aloud in her happiness. And suddenly she remembered the name of the angel and spoke it aloud. And all the cottage was filled with a sweet scent as of flowers.

Then the princess remembered all she had been trying to recall, and she knew that the sweet-scented name that she had been seeking was her own heavenly name, and she remembered why she had been sent upon the earth.

THE SWEET-SCENTED NAME

The little peasant girl soon became quite well, and the princess married Maximilian and lived with him happily on the earth until the time came for her to return to her heavenly home and God's eternal kingdom.

Turandina

I

PETER ANTÒNOVITCH BULANIN was spending the summer in the country with the family of his cousin, a teacher of philology. Bulanin himself was a young advocate of thirty years of age, having finished his course at the University only two years before.

The past year had been a comparatively fortunate one. He had successfully defended two criminal cases on the nomination of the Court, as well as a civil case undertaken at the instigation of his own heart. All three cases had been won by his brilliant pleading. The jury had acquitted the young man who had killed his father out of pity because the old man fasted too assiduously and suffered in consequence ; they had acquitted the poor seamstress who had thrown vitriol at the girl her lover wished to marry ; and in the civil court the judge had awarded the plaintiff a hundred and fifty roubles, saying that his rights were indisputable, though the defendant asserted that the sum had previously been paid. For all this good work Peter Antònovitch himself had received only fifteen roubles, this money having been paid to him by the man who had received the hundred and fifty.

But, as will be understood, one cannot live a whole year on fifteen roubles, and Peter Antònovitch had to fall back on his own resources, that is, on the money his father sent him from home. As far as the law was concerned there was as yet nothing for him but fame.

But his fame was not at present great, and as his receipts from his father were but moderate Peter Antònovitch often fell into a despondent and elegiac mood. He looked on life rather pessimistically, and captivated young ladies by the eloquent pallor of his face and by the sarcastic utterances which he gave forth on every possible occasion.

One evening, after a sharp thunder-storm had cleared and refreshed the air, Peter Antònovitch went out for a walk alone. He wandered along the narrow field-paths until he found himself far from home.

A picture of entrancing beauty stretched

itself out before him, canopied by the bright-blue dome of heaven besprinkled with scattered cloudlets and illumined by the soft and tender rays of the departing sun. The narrow path by which he had come led along the high bank of a stream rippling along in the winding curves of its narrow bed—the shallow water of the stream was transparent and gave a pleasant sense of cool freshness. It looked as if one need only step into it to be at once filled with the joy of simple happiness, to feel as full of life and easy grace of movement as the rosy-bodied boys bathing there.

Not far away were the shades of the quiet forest ; beyond the river lay an immense semi-circular plain, dotted here and there with woods and villages, a dusty ribbon of a road curving snake-like across it. On the distant horizon gleamed golden stars, the crosses of far-away churches and belfries shining in the sunlight.

Everything looked fresh and sweet and simple, yet Peter Antònovitch was sad. And it seemed to him that his sadness was but intensified by the beauty around ; as if some evil tempter were seeking to allure him to evil by some entrancing vision.

For to Peter Antònovitch all this earthly

beauty, all this enchantment of the eyes, all this delicate sweetness pouring itself into his young and vigorous body, was only as a veil of golden tissue spread out by the devil to hide from the simple gaze of man the impurity, the imperfection, and the evil of Nature.

This life, adorning itself in beauty and breathing forth perfumes, was in reality, thought Peter Antònovitch, only the dull prosaic iron chain of cause and effect—the burdensome slavery from which mankind could never get free.

Tortured by such thoughts Peter Antònovitch had often felt himself as unhappy as if in him there had awakened the soul of some ancient monster who had howled piteously outside the village at night. And now he thought :

" If only a fairy-tale could come into one's life and for a time upset the ordered arrangement of pre-determined Fate ! Oh, fairy-tale, fashioned by the wayward desires of men who are in captivity to life and who cannot be reconciled to their captivity— sweet fairy-tale, where art thou ? "

He remembered an article he had read the day before in a magazine, written by the Minister of Education ; some words in it had specially haunted his memory. The article spoke of the old fairy-tale tradition of the forest enchantress, Turandina. She had loved a shepherd and had left for him her enchanted home, and with him had lived some happy years on earth until she had been recalled by the mysterious voices of the forest. She had gone away, but the happy years had remained as a grateful memory to mankind.

Peter Antònovitch gave himself up to the fancy—oh for the fairy-tale, for a few enchanted years, a few days . . . ! And he cried aloud and said :

" Turandina, where art thou ? "

II

The sun was low down in the sky. The calm of even had fallen on the spreading fields. The neighbouring forest was hushed. No sound was heard, the air was still, and the grass still sparkling with raindrops was motionless.

It was a moment when the desires of a man fulfil themselves, the one moment which perhaps comes once in his life to every man. It seemed that all around was waiting in a tension of expectation.

TURANDINA

Looking before him into the shining misty vapour, Peter Antònovitch cried again :

" Turandina, where art thou ? "

And under the spell of the silence that encompassed him, his own separate individual will became one with the great universal Will, and with great power and authority he spoke as only once in his life a man has power to speak :

" Turandina, come ! "

And in a sweet and gentle voice he heard the answer :

" I am here."

Peter Antònovitch trembled and looked about. Everything seemed again quite ordinary and his soul was as usual the soul of a poor human being, separate from the universal Soul—he was again an ordinary man, just like you and me, who dwell in days and hours of time. Yet before him stood she whom he had called.

She was a beautiful maiden, wearing a narrow circlet of gold upon her head, and dressed in a short white garment. Her long plaits of hair came below her waist and seemed to have taken to themselves the golden rays of the sunlight. Her eyes, as she gazed intently at the young man, were as blue as if in them a heaven revealed itself, more clear and pure than the skies of earth. Her features were so regular and her hands and feet so well-formed, so perfect were the lines of the figure revealed by the folds of her dress that she seemed an embodiment of perfect maiden loveliness. She would have seemed like an angel from heaven had not her heavy black eyebrows met and so disclosed her witchery; if her skin had not been dark as if tanned by the rays of a burning sun.

Peter Antònovitch could not speak for wonder at her, and she spoke first:

"Thou didst call me and so I came to thee. Thou calledst to me just when I was in need of an earthly shelter in the world of men. Thou wilt take me to thy home. I have nothing of my own except this crown upon my brow, this dress, and this wallet in my hand."

She spoke quietly, so quietly that the tones of her voice could not have been heard above earthly sounds. But so clear was her speech and so tender its tone that even the most indifferent man would have been touched by the least sound of her voice.

When she spoke about going home with him and of her three possessions, Peter

18

TURANDINA

Antònovitch saw that she held in her hand a little bag of red leather drawn together by a golden cord—a very simple and beautiful little bag; something like those in which ladies carry their opera-glasses to the theatre.

Then he asked :

" And who art thou ? "

" I am Turandina, the daughter of King Turandon. My father loved me greatly, but I did that which was not for me to do—out of simple curiosity I disclosed the future of mankind. For this my father was displeased with me and drove me from his kingdom. Some day I shall be forgiven and recalled to my father's home. But now for a time I must dwell among men, and to me have been given these three things : a golden crown, the sign of my birth ; a white garment, my poor covering ; and this wallet, which contains all that I shall need. It is good that I have met with thee. Thou art a man who defendeth the unhappy, and who devoteth his life to the triumph of Truth among men. Take me with thee to thy home ; thou wilt never regret thy deed."

Peter Antònovitch did not know what to do or what to think. One thing was clear :

this maiden, dressed so lightly, speaking so strangely, must be sheltered by him; he could not leave her alone in the forest, far from any human dwelling.

He thought she might be a runaway, hiding her real name and inventing some unlikely story. Perhaps she had escaped from an asylum, or from her own home.

There was nothing in her face or in her appearance, however, except her scanty clothing and her words, to indicate anything strange in her mind. She was perfectly quiet and calm. If she called herself Turandina it was doubtless because she had heard some one mention the name, or she might even have read the fairy-story of Turandina.

III

With such thoughts in his mind Peter Antònovitch said to the beautiful unknown :

" Very well, dear young lady, I will take you home with me. But I ought to warn you that I do not live alone, and therefore I advise you to tell me your real name. I'm afraid that my relatives will not believe that you are the daughter of King Turandon. As far as I know there is no such king at the present time."

TURANDINA

Turandina smiled as she said :

" I have told thee the truth, whether thy people believe it or not. It is sufficient for me that thou shouldst believe. And if thou believest me, thou wilt defend me from all evil and from all unhappiness, for thou art a man who hast chosen for thyself the calling in which thou canst uphold the truth and defend the weak."

Peter Antònovitch shrugged his shoulders.

" If you persist in this story," answered he, " I must wash my hands of the matter, and I cannot be answerable for any possible consequences. Of course I will take you home with me until you can find a more suitable place, and I will do all I can to help you. But as a lawyer I very strongly advise you not to hide your real name."

Turandina listened to him with a smile, and when he stopped speaking she said :

" Do not be at all anxious ; everything will be well. Thou wilt see that I shall bring happiness to thee if thou canst show me kindness and love. And do not speak to me so much about my real name. I have spoken the truth to thee, and more I may not say, it is forbidden me to tell thee all. Take me home with thee. Night is coming on ; I have journeyed far and am in need of rest."

" Peter Antònovitch was quick to apologise.

" Ah, pardon me, please. I am sorry that this is such an out-of-the-way place; it's quite impossible to get a carriage."

He began to walk in the direction of his home, and Turandina went with him. She did not walk as though she were tired; her feet seemed hardly to touch the ground, though they had to walk over stiff clay and sharp stones, and the moist grass and rain-soaked pathway did not seem to soil her little feet.

When they reached the high bank of the river and could see the first houses of the village, Peter Antònovitch glanced uneasily at his companion and said somewhat awkwardly:

" Pardon me, dear young lady . . ."

Turandina looked at him, and with a little frown interrupted him, saying reproachfully:

" Hast thou forgotten who I am and what is my name? I am Turandina, and not ' dear young lady.' I am the daughter of King Turandon."

" Your pardon, please, Mademoiselle Turandina — it is a very beautiful name, though it is never used now — I wanted to ask you a question."

TURANDINA

" Why dost thou speak so to me ? "
asked Turandina, interrupting him once
more. " Speak not as to one of the young
ladies of thy acquaintance. Say ' thou ' to
me, and address me as a true knight would
speak to his fair lady."

She spoke with such insistence and
authority that Peter Antònovitch felt com-
pelled to obey. And when he turned to
Turandina and for the first time spoke to
her intimately and called her by her name,
he at once felt more at ease.

" Turandina, hast thou not a dress to
wear ? My people would expect thee to wear
an ordinary dress."

Turandina smiled once more and said :

" I don't know. Is'nt my one garment
enough ? I was told that in this wallet I
should find everything that I should need
in the world of men. Take it and look
within ; perhaps thou wilt find there what
thou desirest."

With these words she held out to him her
little bag. And as he pulled apart the cord
and opened it, Peter Antònovitch thought
to himself, " It will be good if some one has
put in some kind of frock for her."

He put his hand into the wallet and feeling
something soft he drew out a small parcel,

so small that Turandina could have closed her hand over it. And when he unwrapped the parcel, there was just what he wanted, a dress such as most young girls were wearing at that time.

He helped Turandina to put it on, and he fastened it for her, for, of course, it buttoned at the back.

" Is that all right now ? " asked Turandina.

Peter Antònovitch looked regretfully at the little bag. It looked much too small to hold a pair of shoes. But he put in his hand again and thought, " A pair of sandals would do nicely."

His fingers touched a little strap, and he drew forth a tiny pair of golden sandals. And then he dried her feet and put on the sandals and fastened the straps for her.

" Now is everything all right ? " asked Turandina again.

There was such a humility in her voice and gesture as she spoke that Peter Antònovitch felt quite happy. It would be quite easy to manage her now, he thought. So he said, " Oh yes ; we can get a hat later on."

TURANDINA

IV

And so there came a fairy-story into the life of a man. Of course, it seemed sometimes as if the young lawyer's life were quite unsuited for such a thing. His relatives were utterly unable to believe the account their young guest gave of herself, and even Peter Antònovitch himself lacked faith. Many times he begged Turandina to tell him her real name, and he played various tricks on her to trap her into confessing that her story was not really true. But Turandina was never angry at his persistence. She smiled sweetly and simply, and with great patience said over and over again :

" I have told you the truth."

" But where is the land over which King Turandon reigns ? " Peter Antònovitch would ask.

" It is far away," Turandina would answer, " and yet if you wish it, it is near also. But none of you can go thither. Only we who have been born in the enchanted kingdom of King Turandon can ever get to that wonderful country."

" But can you not show me how to go there ? " asked Peter Antònovitch.

" No, I cannot," answered Turandina.

" And can you return yourself ? " said he.

" Now, I cannot," said she, " but when my father calls me, I shall return."

There was no sadness in her voice and expression, nor any joy, as she spoke of her expulsion from the enchanted land and of her return. Her voice was always calm and gentle. She looked on all she saw with inquiring eyes, as if seeing everything for the first time, but with a quiet calmness, as if knowing that she would soon become accustomed to all new and strange things, and would easily recognise them again. When she once knew a thing she never made a mistake nor confused it with anything else. All ordinary rules of conduct that people told her or that she herself noticed, were lightly and easily followed, as if she had been accustomed to them from her childhood. She remembered names and faces of people after having once seen them.

Turandina never quarrelled with any one, and she never said anything untrue. When she was advised to use the ordinary Society evasions she shook her head and said :

" One must never say what is untrue. The earth hears everything."

At home and in the company of others Turandina behaved with such dignity and graciousness that all who could believe in a fairy - tale were obliged to believe that they were in the presence of a beautiful princess, the daughter of a great and wise king.

But the fairy-tale was somewhat difficult to reconcile with the ordinary life of the young lawyer and his people. There was a perpetual struggle between the two, and many difficulties arose in consequence.

V

When Turandina had been living with the family for a few days, an official came to the house and said to the servant :

" They say there's a young lady visitor here. She must send in her passport and have it signed."

The servant told her mistress, who spoke to her husband about the matter. He asked Peter Antònovitch about the passport, and the latter went to find Turandina and ask her. Turandina was sitting on the verandah reading a book with much enjoyment.

" Turandina," said Peter Antònovitch, going out to her. " The police have sent to ask for your passport. It must be sent to be signed."

THE SWEET-SCENTED NAME

Turandina listened very attentively to what Peter Antònovitch had to say. And then she asked :

" What is a passport ? "

" Oh, a passport," said he, " don't you know, is — a passport. A paper on which is written your name and your father's name, your age, your rank. You can't possibly live anywhere without a passport."

" If it's necessary," said Turandina calmly, " then, of course, it ought to be in my little bag. Look, there's the bag, take it and see if the passport is inside."

And in the wonderful little bag there was found a passport—a small book in a brown cover, which had been obtained in the province of Astrakhan, in which was inscribed the name of the Princess Tamara Timofeevna Turandon, seventeen years of age, and unmarried. Everything was in order : the seal, the official signature, the signature of the princess herself, and so on, just as in all passport books.

Peter Antònovitch looked at Turandina and smiled :

" So that's who you are," said he, " you are a princess, and your name is Tamara."

But Turandina shook her head.

" No," said she, " I've never been called

Tamara. That passport doesn't tell the truth ; it's only for the police and for those people who do not know and cannot know the truth. I am Turandina, the daughter of King Turandon. Since I have lived in this world I have learnt that people here don't want to know the truth. I don't know anything about the passport. Whoever put it in my little bag must have known that I should need it. But for thee, my word should be enough."

After the passport had been signed Turandina was known as the princess, or Tamara Timofeevna, but her own people continued to call her Turandina.

VI

Her own people—for they came to be her own people. The fairy-tale came into a man's life, and as often happens in a fairy-tale, so it now occurred in life. Peter Antònovitch fell in love with Turandina and Turandina loved him also. He made up his mind to marry her, and this led to slight difficulties in the family.

The teacher-cousin and his wife said :

" In spite of her mysterious origin and her obstinate silence about her family, your

Turandina is a very dear girl, beautiful, intelligent, very good and capable, and well brought up. In short, she is everything that one could wish. But you ought to remember that you have no money, and neither has she.

" It will be difficult for two people to live in Petersburg on the money your father allows you.

" Especially with a princess.

" You must remember that in spite of her sweet ways she's probably accustomed to live in good style.

" She has very small soft hands. True, she has been very modest here, and you say she was barefoot when you met her first and had very little clothing. But we don't know what kind of garments she will want to wear in a town."

Peter Antònovitch himself was rather pessimistic at first. But by and by he remembered how he had found a dress for Turandina in the little bag. A bold thought came into his mind, and he smiled and said :

" I found a house - frock for Turandina in her little bag. Perhaps if I were to rummage in it again I might find a ball-dress for her."

But the teacher's wife, a kind young

woman with a genius for housekeeping, said :

" Much better if you could find some money. If only she had five hundred roubles we could manage to get her a good trousseau."

" We ought to find five hundred thousand —for a princess's dowry," said Peter Antònovitch, laughing.

" Oh, a hundred thousand would be quite enough for you," laughed his cousin in reply.

Just then Turandina came quietly up the steps leading from the garden, and Peter Antònovitch called to her and said :

" Turandina, show me your little bag, dear. Perhaps you have a hundred thousand roubles there."

Turandina held out her little bag to him and said :

" If it's necessary, you will find it in the bag."

And Peter Antònovitch again put his hand into the little bag and drew forth a large packet of notes. He began to count them, but without counting he could see they represented a large quantity of money.

VII

So this great fairy-tale came into the young man's life. And though it didn't seem well suited to the taking-in of a fairy-tale, yet room was found for it somewhere. The fairy-tale bought a place in his life—with its own charm and the treasures of the enchanted bag.

Turandina and the young lawyer were married. And Turandina had first a little son and then a daughter. The boy was like his mother, and grew up to be a gentle dreamy child. The girl was like her father, gay and intelligent.

And so the years went by. Every summer, when the days were at their longest, a strange melancholy overshadowed Turandina. She used to go out in the mornings to the edge of the forest and stand there listening to the forest voices. And after some time she would walk home again slowly and sadly.

And once, standing there at midday, she heard a loud voice calling to her :

" Turandina, come. Your father has forgiven you."

And so she went away and never returned. Her little son was then seven years old and her daughter three.

TURANDINA

Thus the fairy-tale departed from this life and never came back. But Turandina's little son never forgot his mother.

Sometimes he would wander away by himself so as to be quite alone. And when he came home again there was such an expression upon his face that the teacher's wife said to her husband in a whisper :

" He has been with Turandina."

Lohengrin

I

MASHENKA PESTRYÀKOVA was a young and pretty girl, dreamy in temperament, and by no means intellectual. Her nose was a little upturned, her eyes grey and vivacious, and in the Spring she had freckles on her cheeks, under her eyes, and on her nose. She lived with her mother and brother in Pea Street, in the same house in which Oblomof once lived. She taught in a sort of private school, and received her meagre salary at irregular intervals. She was very fond of going to the opera, and liked best of all to hear Wagner.

Mashenka's mother had a small pension, which she augmented by selling some books on commission and by letting apartments. They gave up three rooms of their house in this way and used the rest themselves. The little brother went to school every day, and Mashenka helped him with his lessons in the evening and gave part of her salary to her mother.

Mashenka often let her thoughts wander into vague and pleasant reveries. Sometimes these reveries would take a more definite form, and the sweet image of her dream would be identified with one or other of her youthful acquaintances. Then for a while meetings with the new friend would be very agreeable to her. But the friendship never lasted very long.

The reality was always disappointing. The actual happening was so different from her own beautiful vision of life. Instead of listening to passionate glowing words like those which sound so attractive in the pages of a novel and are so charming when sung by Sobinof on the stage of the Marinsky Theatre—so different from the usual sounds of life in Pea Street—her companion would speak in a dull and prosaic way about their own doings or those of their neighbours, would utter words about money, words of blame, envious sneers, spiteful gossip, sometimes even compliment her in an embarrassing way. Then the dear figure of her dream would grow dim and become no longer attractive, and there would be days when Mashenka didn't want to dream about anything or anybody; she would only feel apathetic and bored. Then she would look forward to the next meeting. And next time she would be disappointed again.

And yet in spite of this some one did come and take possession of Mashenka's soul—a rather ugly young man, short and awkward, and delicate in health, with weak eyes that seemed to blink continuously, thin reddish hair, meagre reddish whiskers, and scanty beard. He dressed himself neatly and carefully, wore a cornelian stone ring on his finger and a pearl pin in his mauve or green necktie, but his dress showed neither special taste nor abundance of means.

For a long time Mashenka did not know his real name nor his occupation. She called him by a strange nickname—taken from the opera,—Lohengrin.

" My Lohengrin is coming to-day," she used to say to her mother.

" That's your Lohengrin's ring," her mother would say when they heard a timid, uncertain little sound from the door-bell.

" Your Lohengrin's a silly," said her little brother Serezha frankly. He liked to tease Mashenka sometimes. Only occasionally, of course. He was only twelve years old, and just a little afraid of his sister.

LOHENGRIN

At first Mashenka called her friend Lohengrin because she met him first in the gallery of the Marinsky Theatre one evening when *Lohengrin* was being performed. And afterwards there were other reasons why he still kept so strange a nickname.

II

Mashenka had gone to the theatre that evening with a girl friend and two student-acquaintances. "Lohengrin" sat behind her, just a little to one side, and before the beginning of the second act Mashenka noticed that he was looking at her very intently. She began to feel awkward, and looked round angrily at the young man.

She did not much like the look of him. His persistent gaze seemed rude and tiresome. And she disliked him still more when, after turning on him for the second time a more severe glance and a more decided frown, the young man averted his gaze with such guilty haste that it seemed to her he must be accustomed to stare rudely at people and then suddenly turn away.

She wanted to point him out to her companions and ask whether they knew the young man, but just then the orchestra

37

began to play, and every one was silent. Mashenka, under the spell of the incomparable music, quickly forgot all about the tiresome person behind her.

In the next *entr'acte* Mashenka walked up and down the corridor with her friends, and did not think of the young man until she became conscious that he was walking behind and staring at her. For a long time afterwards she felt his gaze upon her neck, just on the line where the bare neck shows between the top of the white collar and the hair above it. It was so annoying and embarrassing that she didn't know what to do.

The *entr'acte* was at an end, and they were all crowding back through the narrow doors when Mashenka took advantage of the general noise and confusion to say to the student beside her :

" Do you know the young man next to us ? His seat is just behind ours."

She spoke in a low voice so that the young man behind should not hear. But the student looked round and said aloud :

" No, I don't know him. Why do you ask ? "

It was a little difficult to reply.

" He stares at me all the time," she whispered.

38

" You've made a conquest of him," said the student calmly, still speaking loudly.

When they were in their places again and preparing to listen, Mashenka for some reason or other felt vexed that the student had treated the matter so lightly. As if to spite him she looked attentively at the young man behind, and thought to herself with a condescending pity :

" Poor thing ! Perhaps he thinks himself handsome and irresistible."

A faint smile played about her lips, and she noticed with some satisfaction that the young man blushed a little, and that in his eyes there was a gleam of pleasure. But she quickly recollected herself and frowned again, looked angrily at him, and turned away, thinking :

" He's no business to think anything of himself. He's quite ugly."

In the third *entr'acte* he walked behind her again, not at all disconcerted, though somewhat timid and confused, looking like an amusing reddish-coloured shadow stealing along the wall.

After the opera was over Mashenka saw him again while she was putting on her cloak. He was evidently hurrying to get out before she did, and was already dressed in a long coat with an astrakhan collar and a fur hat. He stood and looked across at her, searching through the crowd as if boring through it with his pointed beetle-like whiskers—looked at her with a sadly strange and furtive glance, as if he wished to notice particularly and remember every little fold of her dress and her cloak.

Once more Mashenka felt vexed and awkward, and she made up her mind not to tell any one about this young man.

" Nuisance ! " said she angrily to herself.

III

Mashenka went home with a whole crowd of young people, all talking and laughing gaily. She tried hard not to look behind her, but she was certain that the young man was following them. She didn't want to hear it, and yet she found herself listening involuntarily to the light footfall—a cautious, stealthy tread.

When she said good-bye to her friends at the gate, Mashenka saw the stranger once more. He went quietly past the house, crossed over to the other side of the road, and turned back in the direction from which they had come.

LOHENGRIN

The clumsy dvornik, wearing an immense shaggy overcoat and his cap pulled low down over his forehead and ears, flung open the creaking little door in the heavy gate. Mashenka's companions, still talking noisily all together, went away up the street. Mashenka went into the yard, and the little door was slammed behind her. She waited by the gate and listened.

Some one came along with stealthy little steps, stopped outside, and began to speak in a whisper to the dvornik. The latter muttered something indistinctly, as if unwilling to answer, but presently Mashenka heard him thanking the other for something, and then he went on talking. She tried hard to hear what was said, but could not catch a word, partly at first because they spoke so softly, but afterwards she was too much overwhelmed with confusion to listen ; her heart beat rapidly, the blood coursed through her veins and drummed in her ears.

There was not much sleep for Mashenka that night. In her dreams she saw the beautiful knight, the bright-haired Lohengrin in shining armour, and heard his voice :

" I am Lohengrin, thy champion knight from heaven."

Then the features and the whole figure of Lohengrin became strangely altered. An unhealthy-looking little man with reddish beetle-like whiskers, his fur hat pushed to the back of his head, his little red ears almost hidden by the fur collar of his overcoat, waving his hands awkwardly in his grey fur gloves, slipping in his shiny galoshes on the icy pavement of Pea Street, sang these same words. His voice was as sweet and melodious as that of the stage Lohengrin, and yet it sounded a little ridiculous and repulsive.

IV

After that evening Mashenka met the young man every day as she was going home from school. He walked behind her like a tiresome and amusing shadow from which she could not escape, and accompanied her to the very door of her home. Sometimes he even entered the gate of the courtyard and came up the outside staircase, and when Mashenka went indoors and slammed the door behind her she felt that he was still waiting outside. Her heart beat quickly, her cheeks crimsoned, her eyes glistened as she smiled to herself and thought :

LOHENGRIN

" Who can he be, this red-haired Lohengrin ? "

But at length she began to get tired of it. One day when Lohengrin was walking close behind her in the street Mashenka turned sharply round, went up to him, and said :

" What is it you want ? Why do you follow me every day ? "

Her cheeks were crimson and her voice trembled a little as she spoke ; her hands, gloved and hidden away inside her muff, were hot and shaking. It seemed to her that even her shoulders under her thick winter dress must be shaking and crimson too, and that a fever of trembling ran through her whole body.

The eyes of the young man looked guiltily away from her. He raised his hat, then put it on again, and bowing awkwardly, began to speak in a pleasant though slightly hoarse voice, as if he had a cold.

" I beg your pardon, please forgive me, Marya Constantìnovna."

" However do you know my name ? " cried Mashenka angrily.

She was astonished to find that the young man's voice, which she heard now for the first time, had in it a slight reminiscence of the voice of the singer who had taken the part of Lohengrin in the theatre—the same Russian tone and the same gentle sweetness. It would even have sounded more like it if it had not been so unpleasantly hoarse.

"I learnt your name from the dvornik of your house, Marya Constantìnovna," answered the young man. "I had no means of getting to know it otherwise, as I have no friends who are acquainted with you."

"That means, I suppose, that you asked the dvornik all about me," said Mashenka in a tone of annoyance. "It was a nice occupation for you, I must say."

But the young man was not at all abashed.

"Yes, I asked him about you and about your honoured mother and your nice little brother. I got all the information on the evening when I first met you."

"But why did you want to know about us?" asked Mashenka.

Not noticing what she was doing the girl turned and walked again in the direction of her home, and the red-haired young man walked by her side. He answered her with a strange circumstantiality.

"Of course you yourself understand,

44

LOHENGRIN

Marya Constantìnovna, that in the present day one needs to be very particular in making new acquaintances," said he. " One can't make friends with everybody one meets ; one ought to know beforehand something of the person one is dealing with."

" Yes, indeed," said Mashenka with a laugh. " Please be particular and don't try to get acquainted with me."

" Pardon me, Marya Constantìnovna," replied the young man seriously, " but that would be quite impossible."

" What would be impossible ? " asked the young girl in astonishment.

" It is impossible for me not to get to know you," answered the young man quietly, " because at our first meeting at the opera when *Lohengrin* was being played—if you will allow me to remind you of that night— you made such an indelible impression on me that I felt at once that I loved you with a great and wonderful love. And so I couldn't help following you and getting to know all I could about you from the dvornik at your door."

Mashenka smiled and said :

" But it's no use your taking the trouble to find out about me. I have quite enough friends as it is, and I don't need any more. It's not very nice for me to have you continually following me, and as you seem to be a respectable young man, I ask you now not to do so any more. I shouldn't like any of my friends to notice it and think badly of me."

The young man walking beside her listened attentively to what she said, and did not try to interrupt her. When she had finished it seemed as if he thought he had given her an answer, and Mashenka suddenly thought to herself :

" Now he will raise his hat and go away and never try to see me any more."

And this thought, which should have soothed and calmed her, somehow made her feel suddenly annoyed and sad about something — as if she had become quite accustomed to her silent, ugly, awkward companion and didn't want him to leave her. However he acted quite differently from what she had thought. He did raise his hat, but only to say :

" Allow me, Marya Constantìnovna, to have the honour of introducing myself to you—Nikolai Stepanovitch Sklonyaef."

Mashenka shrugged her shoulders.

" It's no use your introducing yourself,"

said she. " What makes you think I want to know you ? Haven't I just told you that I am not on the look-out for any new acquaintances ? "

The young man looked timidly into her eyes as he answered :

" Marya Constantìnovna, don't send me away from you. I won't ask you anything just now, but because I love you so that I cannot imagine how I could have lived before without knowing you, please let me have at least the hope that when you understand how great is my love you also may begin to love me in return."

" What foolishness ! " cried Mashenka. " A perfectly unknown young man comes up to me in the street and talks like this ! And what am I to do ? Why should I listen to you ? Please go away at once."

V

Mashenka walked on quickly, but her companion did not go away. He spoke to her in words which vexed and confused her. Still looking into her eyes with a timid and cautious gaze he said :

" Marya Constantìnovna, please allow me to remind you that it may often happen that people who were previously unacquainted with one another suddenly become very good friends."

" Yes, but not in the street," said Mashenka, and now she laughed outright.

There was nothing to laugh at, of course, and Mashenka quickly recollected herself and bit her pretty full red underlip with her strong little white teeth. It seemed to her that her laugh only encouraged this importunate young man.

But he said in a beseeching tone :

" For mercy's sake, Marya Constantìnovna, and why not in the street ? Isn't it all the same ? If a man is truly in love, believe me, Marya Constantìnovna, all outward circumstances and worldly conventions cease to exist for him ; he cannot think of anything else except the object of his passionate affection."

Saying this, he pressed both his hands on his heart and then waved his left hand in the air exactly as the singer in the opera had done when he sang the declaration of Lohengrin.

Mashenka could not possibly take him seriously. She even felt a little disappointed that the adventure had nothing in it to frighten her — it was simply amusing. She was a little sorry for the young man, so persistent, so incoherent in his speech. She smiled as she listened and thought to herself :

" What a red-headed Lohengrin he is, talking of love in this way ! "

But he went on :

" And because my intentions are entirely honourable and exalted, I myself do not wish to meet you in the streets or in any public place, or in a private room in a restaurant. And I should be very greatly obliged, Marya Constantìnovna, if you would do me the great honour to present me to your respected mother."

" What more will you want ? " exclaimed Mashenka. " How could I present you to my mother ? She would be sure to ask me where I met you first. Please go away now or I shall really be angry."

She laughed again, however, and the young man went on :

" Do not be angry with me, Marya Constantìnovna. I shall do nothing to offend you, and if after some time you cannot feel any inclination towards me, then I will not venture to disturb you any more, but will go away into the shadow of my own poor life and only watch from afar your happiness with another, more worthy than I of your love."

His little nose got red, his small, restless blinking eyes reddened also, and he twisted his small body so that he seemed smaller than ever and looked as if he were just going to weep.

Mashenka considered the situation and tried hard to keep a good opinion of herself as she thought :

" Now, how can I send him away ! It's impossible not to feel sorry for such a man. I can't complain to a passer-by or call a policeman."

It was pleasant to think some one had fallen in love with her. All the young men who had paid her attentions before had either not been serious or they themselves had been odious to her. But this man was so humble and spoke with such an engaging eloquence ; he simply would not leave her side, and his words reminded her of the love speeches of viscounts and marquises in a novel.

She tried to look sternly at him as she asked sharply :

" Well, and who are you ? "

" I am a man who is in love with you," answered Lohengrin.

LOHENGRIN

" Yes, you've told me that before," said Mashenka, " but I want to know who you are and what is your occupation."

The thought suddenly came to her that by so speaking she was giving the young man some hope of getting to know her. She felt vexed with herself. But her companion answered :

" Pardon me, Marya Constantìnovna, why is it necessary for you to know that ? "

" Ah, that's quite true," said Mashenka, " it's nothing at all to do with me. I hope you'll go away now."

But his answer had really made her angry, and this added to her former vexation. She suddenly wished to make him see that she had a right to question him, and not being able to master this imprudent desire, she continued :

" Well, you say that you want me to introduce you to my mother ; how can I do that without knowing ? Shall I say to her, ' Mother, this is a man who has fallen in love with me ! ' "

" Yes, just that," said he.

" What foolishness ! " said Mashenka. " How is that possible ? "

" Why is it not possible if it's the truth," said Lohengrin.

VI

When the time came for them to cross the street, Lohengrin took Mashenka by the arm. She looked at him with some surprise, but did not draw herself away. Looking cautiously round so as to avoid the traffic, he silently led her across the road, now covered with a thin layer of dirty brownish snow, and striped with the marks of carriage wheels. When they reached the pavement he dropped her arm and walked alone.

She went on with the conversation.

" No, it's impossible. That's not the way such things are done, and after all, what need is there to introduce you to my mother ? "

" Believe me, Marya Constantìnovna," answered the young man, " I quite understand that you would like to know my occupation and my social position, and if I do not tell you all about it just now it is for very serious reasons. I have vowed not to disclose these matters for certain worldly considerations, and I cannot tell you for fear of unpleasant consequences."

" What foolishness ! " said Mashenka again.

" No, Marya Constantìnovna," said he.

LOHENGRIN

" Do not say that. You remember the opera where I had the honour of seeing you for the first time. Lohengrin should remind you that it is sometimes necessary to conceal the truth until the right moment. You saw how imprudent the beautiful but inquisitive Elsa was, beseeching her husband to tell her his secret and disclose his name and calling, and you saw how cruelly she was punished. Certainly she repented of it afterwards, but, as they say, if your head is off it's no use weeping for the loss of your hair."

" Oh yes, indeed," put in Mashenka, " you and I are certainly very much like Lohengrin and Elsa."

Her sarcastic tone did not disconcert her companion. He answered :

" You, Marya Constantìnovna, are incomparably more beautiful and good than was the lady Elsa, and so if I do not dare to liken myself to Lohengrin, yet all the same, taken together, we can be compared with them. It is true that knights in armour have gone out of fashion in our day, but the knightly feelings remain ; love burns in the hearts of emotional people no less clear than in former times. Our lives may appear dull and barren, but in reality they are no less wonderful and mysterious than was the life of Lohengrin and Elsa when he came down the stream to her, borne by the silver-winged swan."

" Ah, Lohengrin ! " exclaimed Mashenka, mockingly, yet perhaps a little touched.

The young man looked at her and waited for her to say more. But Mashenka was silent and said no more until she reached her home. Then she stood still for a moment and looked in the young man's eyes.

" What am I to do with you, Mr. Lohengrin ? You must go home or about your mysterious business. It's not convenient for you to come in just now."

His answering gaze was one of happiness and confusion, and so much hope that Mashenka felt obliged to say :

" Well, come to-morrow evening at eight o'clock. I will tell mother. I don't know what she'll say to me, but I daresay she will receive you."

VII

So Mashenka went indoors to tell her mother what had happened and to prepare her for the young man's visit on the morrow. The mother grumbled a little.

" What's all this, Mashenka," said she.

LOHENGRIN

" You surely don't think it's possible to have a man in from the street. Who knows what he may have in mind; it's quite likely he's a rogue of some kind."

But after a little while she came to the conclusion :

" Well, I suppose we'd better see him and know what he's after."

So Lohengrin came at the appointed time, brought a box of sweetmeats, stayed an hour and a half, drank tea, behaved very respectfully to the mother, joked with school-boy Serezha, amused Mashenka with his rhetorical phrases, and took his departure before any of them had time to get bored.

After he had gone the mother asked Mashenka :

" Well, who is he really ? "

" Indeed, mother, I've told you everything I know about him. I don't know anything more. I only know him as Lohengrin. His name is Nikolai Stepanovitch Sklonyaef, but what he does I don't know. He's just Lohengrin."

" You'd better look in the Directory to-morrow when you go to school," said her mother, " and find his name. By his talk and his manners he's quite all right, but you never can tell. No one knows anything about him and there may be something under the surface. You must find out all about him."

So on the next day Mashenka looked through the Directory, but she couldn't find anybody of the name of Sklonyaef. She began to think that there could be no such name and that Lohengrin had made it up himself.

However, he continued to visit them, bringing sometimes a bunch of flowers, sometimes a box of chocolates. He no longer tried to meet Mashenka in the street ; when they met it was quite accidentally.

When he came the second time Mashenka asked him why his name was not in the Directory.

He was not in the least confused— Mashenka was surprised to find that in spite of his timid ways, his blinking eyes, and his ingratiating manner, this strange young man was generally self-possessed and very rarely put out of countenance—

" I've only lately come to Petersburg," said he, " and my name is not in the Directory yet. I expect it will be in next year."

He laughed as he spoke, and Mashenka felt sure that he was not speaking the truth.

"But where do you live?" asked she. "What do you do for a living? Where do you work?"

But Lohengrin made reply:

"Pardon me, Marya Constantìnovna, I cannot tell you anything about my address or my occupation."

"And why not?" asked Mashenka in wonder.

"Because, as I have already had the honour of telling you, Marya Constantìnovna, I have important reasons for keeping these matters a profound secret."

Mashenka thought for a moment or two and then said:

"But listen a moment. This is all very strange. At first I thought you were simply joking; but if you are in earnest, then it's all stranger than ever."

"I am not joking at all," said he; "but more than that I also trust that when you love me it will be for myself alone, not considering who I may be nor what is my occupation."

"And if I don't love you?" asked Mashenka with a smile.

"Then I shall vanish from the field of your vision," said he, "as Lohengrin did, when he floated away in that wonderful boat drawn down the many-watered Rhine by the silver-winged swan."

" Oh, Lohengrin," laughed Mashenka once more.

VIII

Mashenka laughed. She was getting used to speak of him as Lohengrin. Everybody called him that now.

Mashenka laughed, and yet sometimes she fell into a reverie and dreamed. And in her dreams the beautiful form of the stage Lohengrin, clad in shining armour, singing so sweetly and making his theatrically beautiful stage gestures, blended itself with the form of an unattractive young man wearing a fur cap instead of a helmet, and a starched shirt in place of armour ; speaking eloquently in his hoarse but pleasant-sounding Yaroslavsky tone of voice, and making these same amusingly-triumphant gestures.

" He loves me, poor boy," thought Mashenka, and the thought became more and more pleasant to her.

To believe firmly that you are beloved by another, is it not as if you yourself loved ? And is not love infectious ? Sweet, in-gratiating, enchanting, love spreads a brightly

58

gleaming veil of enchantment over all the objects of its desire.

And so, becoming accustomed little by little to the pleasant thought of being beloved, accustomed to this amusing mixture of the two Lohengrins — one of the opera of the wise magician Wagner, the other of the everyday life in Pea Street—Mashenka felt at length that she was in love. The amusing mystery enveloping his actual life became less of a hindrance to her.

After some time Lohengrin guessed that Mashenka had begun to care for him, and one day he said to her :

" Marya Constantinovna, you can make me the happiest of men—I beg you to consent to be my wife."

Then, as if she were not yet ready to be asked such a question, Mashenka was seized with a profound alarm. The dark and dreadful suspicions sleeping in her soul were roused and they were too strong for her. She looked at Lohengrin in terror and thought :

" Why does he hide his occupation from me — it must be something shameful and contemptible. Perhaps he is a spy or a hangman ! "

Not long before, Mashenka had read in a newspaper an account of a young workman who had hired himself out as a hangman. He was described as a weak and ugly person, and as she read the description of him, she had thought that he must have looked something like her Lohengrin.

" You must tell me first," Mashenka said timidly, " who you are. It's dreadful not to know."

She felt her cheeks grow pale and her lips tremble. She was seated in a deep soft armchair in the corner of the drawing-room, her mother's favourite chair ; it had been in the family longer than any of them could remember, and many remembrances of pleasure and agitation were connected with it. Enveloped in the depths of the large chair, where she could smell the odour of its old material, Mashenka felt herself very small and pitiful ; her hands clasped together on her knees were pale and trembling as if with cold.

Lohengrin reddened a little and was more confused than Mashenka had ever seen him. He stood with his back to the windows, but in the twilight Mashenka watched strange shadows flitting across his face. His eyes blinked continuously, his little red ears twitched, he made strange unsuitable gestures with his hands as he replied :

LOHENGRIN

" Marya Constantìnovna, if the lady Elsa was inquisitive and indiscreet, and if the noble Lohengrin could not withstand her importunity, why need we repeat their fatal mistake ? You were pleased to say, Marya Constantìnovna, that all this is dreadful for you, but why ? I have an extraordinary love for you, a love devouring all my life, a love very rarely met with and only described in old romances, not at all in the works of present-day writers. Loving you with such an unusual love, so ardent that I cannot live without you,—if you refuse me I shall quickly put an end to myself,—I desire, dear Mashenka, that your own love should overcome the terrors you are feeling, and triumph over all that which is at present unknown to you. True and passionate love ought to be stronger even than death itself. So, dear Mashenka, conquer your fears and tell me—do you love me, and will you continue to love me whatever you may afterwards learn about me ? "

Mashenka began to weep. What else could she do ! Tears are so helpful in the various difficulties of life. She fumbled for her handkerchief, but, of course, it was not to be found, and she was obliged to wipe away her tears with the palm of her right

61

hand—the tears which trickled mercilessly down both cheeks and along her little up-turned nose. She wept and said :

" Why, oh why do you wish not to say who you are ? Why do you torture me like this ? Perhaps you do something very bad."

Lohengrin shrugged his shoulders as he answered :

" That depends on how you look at it. To some people my occupation may seem mean and base, and some people may despise me for it. But I do what I know how to do, and you yourself have been able to see what sort of a man I am apart from my work. If you love me you must believe in me, and even if it turned out that I was a loathsome vampire you should follow me to my tomb, for, if I see in you the most beautiful maiden upon earth, the enchanting Lady Elsa, then you, loving me in return, ought to see in me the noble knight Lohengrin, whose father Parsifal is the guardian of the Holy Grail. And though we may live in the prosaic town of Petersburg in one of the most ordinary streets, and not in one of the castles of the knights of old ; though we have to live the ordinary life of every day, and cannot perform the knightly exploits of old time—our destiny has been portioned out to us by

Fate—none of this can alter the passionate feelings of our hearts."

Mashenka still wept, and yet she was able to laugh, too. The eloquence of Lohengrin's plea was full of sweet and tender soothing.

" I am the Princess Elsa," she thought, "and not simply Mashenka. It means that I am indeed what I feel in myself and not what I appear to others. And he, my Lohengrin ! How is it possible for him to be a spy or a conspirator or a hangman ? How dreadful to think of such things ! But whatever he may do I love him all the same —for me he is Lohengrin, and if it is terrible and difficult to live with him, to die with my beloved will be sweet to me."

She got up from her chair, put her arms tenderly round the young man's neck, and still weeping bitterly, exclaimed :

" Lohengrin, my Lohengrin, whoever thou mayest be I love thee. Whithersoever thou wilt lead me I will follow thee. In whatsoever thou doest I will be thy aid—in life and in death. I love thee as thou dost wish, dear Lohengrin. I love thee as maidens loved their knights in the stories of old."

IX

Confident and happy, Lohengrin, the accepted lover of Mashenka, departed. Mashenka still mingled her tears and laughter. Her mother was astonished at the news.

"How can you think of marrying him, Mashenka?" said she. "You don't mean to say you have promised without knowing anything about him? You'll find out suddenly one day that he's an escaped convict or something of that sort."

But Mashenka only blushed, and repeated obstinately:

"It doesn't matter if he's a convict or a spy or even a hangman. I shall be one too, for I love him."

And Serezha whispered in her ear:

"If he is the leader of a robber band ask him to let me be one of his men. I'm small enough to climb through the little windows."

And Mashenka laughed.

But when Lohengrin reached home he resolved that his secret was no longer worth keeping. He put his visiting card into an envelope and posted it to Mashenka.

Next day when she got home from school, Serezha met her and said with an air of mystery:

LOHENGRIN

" There's a letter for you. I expect it's from Lohengrin, arranging to meet you somewhere."

Mashenka ran off to her own room with the letter, tore open the envelope, and found a scrap of cardboard with something printed on it and a few lines of writing in violet ink. Her hands trembled, her eyes grew dim ; it was with difficulty she managed to read the simple words :

NIKOLAI STEPANOVITCH BALKASHIN
SKILLED BOOKBINDER

48 Matthew Street.

And below was written :

I hid my real occupation from you, dear Mashenka, fearing that you might despise an artisan, but now I am no longer afraid, being convinced that your love for me cannot change.

Both Mashenka and her mother rejoiced that the secret held nothing terrible. The mother felt inclined to grumble a little at having a workman for her son-in-law, but allowed herself to be pacified when Mashenka assured her that his bookbinding would be done in an artistic manner, and that this branch of the work could be extended. But

THE SWEET-SCENTED NAME

Serezha was really disappointed; he had dreamed of night expeditions, but there was now no opportunity for him to climb through the windows of houses.

Perhaps Mashenka was a little disappointed also that everything had turned out so simple and ordinary. But in spite of everything Lohengrin would always remain her Lohengrin, and the image of her dream would never fade away; for love is not only stronger than death, but it is able to triumph over the terrible dulness of ordinary everyday life.

Who art Thou ?

I

ONE year follows after another, the centuries pass away, and still to man is never revealed the mystery of the world and the greater mystery of his own soul.

Man seeks and questions, but does not find an answer. Wise men are as children ; they do not know. And there are some people who have not even got so far as to ask the question :

" Who am I ? "

It was the end of May and already hot weather in the large town. In the side-street it was hot and stifling, and still worse in the courtyard. The brownish - red iron roofs of the five - storey stone buildings on each of the four sides of the yard were burning hot, as were also the large cobble-stones of its dirty pavement. A new house was being built at the side, just such another ugly heap of pretension, a modern building with an ugly front. From this building came a pungent smell of lime and dry brick-dust.

Several children were running about in the yard, shrieking and quarrelling. They belonged to the door-keeper, the servants, and the humbler inhabitants of the building. Little twelve-year-old Grishka, the son of Anushka, the cook at No. 17, looked out on them all from the fourth-floor kitchen window. He lay on his stomach in the window-seat, his thin little legs in their short dark-blue knickers, and his bare feet stretched out behind him.

Grishka's mother wouldn't let him go out into the yard this morning; she was in a bad temper. She remembered that Grishka had broken a cup yesterday; and though he had been beaten then as a punishment, she had reminded him of it again this morning.

" You're just spoilt," said she. " There's no need for you to run about in the yard. You'll stay indoors to-day, and you can learn your lessons."

" I haven't got any examination," Grishka reminded her with some pride. And as usual, when he remembered his school triumphs he laughed joyfully. But his mother looked sternly at him and said :

WHO ART THOU ?

" Well, all the same, you'll stay indoors unless you want a whipping. What are you grinning at ? If I were you I shouldn't find anything to laugh about."

Anushka was fond of repeating this phrase —quite enigmatical to Grishka. Ever since her husband's death, which obliged her to go out as a servant, she had looked upon Grishka and herself as unhappy creatures, and when she thought about the child's future she always painted it in dark colours. Grishka ceased to smile and began to feel uncomfortable.

However, he didn't much want to go into the yard. He wasn't dull indoors. He had a picture-book which he hadn't yet read, and he betook himself to that enjoyment. But he didn't read for very long. He climbed up on the window-seat and looked out upon the children in the yard. Presently, trying to forget a slight headache, he let himself dream a little.

To dream—that was Grishka's favourite occupation. He imagined all sorts of things in all sorts of ways, but he himself was always in the centre — he dreamed about himself and the world. When he went to bed Grishka always tried to think of something tender, joyful, a little painful and shameful perhaps, and sometimes dreadful. Then a pleasant feeling stole over him, though the day might have been an unpleasant one. Many unpleasant things often fell to his lot in the day - time, this poor little boy, brought up in the kitchen with his poor, irritable, capricious, discontented mother. But the more unpleasantnesses there were, the pleasanter it was to console himself by his fancies. It was with a mixture of feelings that he snuggled his head into the pillow and imagined terrible things.

When he woke in the morning Grishka never hurried to get up. It was dark and stuffy in the corridor where he slept ; the box on which his bed was made up was not so soft as the spring mattress on the mistress's bed where he had sometimes thrown himself when his mother wasn't looking and the people of the house were away. But all the same it was comfortable and quiet there as long as he didn't remember that it was time to go to school, or on a holiday, until his mother called to him to get up. And this only happened when it was necessary to send him to a shop to buy something, or for him to help in some way. At other times his mother didn't trouble about him, and she was even glad to think he was asleep and not bothering her, not getting in her way or staring at what she was doing.

" It's tiring enough without you," she often said to him.

And so Grishka often lay in bed quite a long time, nestling under the torn wadded quilt covering him both winter and summer, though in summer, and when there was a big fire in the kitchen, it was very hot for him. And again he would dream of something pleasant, joyful, gay, but not at all dreadful.

The most insignificant reasons gave rise to Grishka's varied dreams. Sometimes he had enjoyed reading a story or a fairy tale from some old and torn book, one of those given out by the teacher at school once a week from the school library ; sometimes he remembered a curious episode from a book he had been reading aloud to his mother. Everything that happened, everything heard by him from somebody or other that excited his imagination, set him dreaming and im- agining in his own way.

He went every day to a school in the town and learnt easily but moderately, only— he had no time. There was so much to dream about. Also, whenever his mother was free to sit down with some sewing or knitting, Grishka had to read aloud to her some novel or other. She was very fond of novels, though she had never learnt to read herself, and she liked to listen to stories of adventure, and was greatly attracted by the adventures of Sherlock Holmes and *The Key of Happiness*. But she also listened greedily to old novels of Dickens and Thackeray and Eliot. Anushka got some books to read from her mistress, some from the girl student who lived in No. 14.

Anushka had a good memory for the stories she had heard, and she loved to tell them in detail to her friends—to the seam-stress Dusha, and to the housemaid of the general's wife at No. 3.

And so very often in the evenings, plant-ing his elbows affectedly on the white wooden kitchen table, pressing his thin little chest in his blue cotton shirt up against it, crossing under the table his spindly legs that were too short to reach the floor, Grishka used to read aloud, quickly and clearly, not understanding all he read, but often very much agitated by the love passages. He was much interested in situations of diffi-culty and danger, but still more in the scenes of love or jealousy or tenderness, in caressing words, in words expressing the passion,

72

the torture, and the languor of lovers whose happiness was frustrated by the evil of others.

And most of all in his dreams Grishka pictured to himself beautiful ladies who smiled and were tender and gentle, though occasionally cruel, and graceful, fair-haired, blue-eyed pages. The beautiful ladies had ruby lips, and they kissed so sweetly and smiled so tenderly and spoke so gently, and yet their words were sometimes without mercy; they had soft white hands with long thin fingers—soft hands, though they were sometimes strong and cruel, and they could promise all the joy and pain that one human being can give to another. The sweet young pages all had long golden curls reaching to their shoulders; their blue eyes sparkled; they wore pointed slippers and white silk stockings on their shapely legs. Grishka heard their careless laughter, their rosy lips bloomed tranquilly, the crimson of their cheeks glowed brightly; if there were any tears shed sometimes, they came only from the eyes of the sweet little pages. The ladies themselves, beautiful and merciless as they were, never wept, they could only laugh and caress and torture.

For some days past Grishka had been

occupied in dreaming about some far-off beautiful and happy land in which wise people dwelt—people, of course, quite unlike all those he saw about him in this dull house that seemed to him like a prison, in these stifling roads and side-streets, everywhere in this dull northern metropolis. What sort of people lived in it ? Here were no beautiful and affectionate ladies like those of his dreams, but self-important and rude mistresses and peasant servants, women and girls, noisy, quarrelsome, bad. There were no knights or pages either. No one wore his lady's scarf, and he had never heard of any one fighting giants in order to protect the weak. The gentlemen here were unpleasant and remote, and either rude or contemptuously familiar ; the peasants were also rude, and they were also remote from Grishka, and their simplicity was as dreadful to him and as artful as the incomprehensible complexity of the gentlefolk.

Nothing that Grishka saw in real life pleased him; it all afflicted his tender soul. He even hated his own name. Even when his mother in a rare interval of unexpected tenderness would suddenly begin to call him Grishenka, even this pet name did not please him. But this stupid diminutive

74

WHO ART THOU ?

Grishka, the name everybody called him by—his mother, her mistress, the young ladies, and every one in the yard,—seemed altogether foreign, altogether unsuitable to what he thought himself. It seemed to him sometimes that it would drop from him, as a badly stuck-on label comes off a wine-bottle.

II

Anushka wanted to put a dish on the window-seat. She seized Grishka's thin ankles in her large rough hand and dragged him down, saying in a needlessly rough way :

" You sprawl about everywhere. And even without you there's not enough room, no place to stand anything."

Grishka sprang away. He looked with frightened eyes at the stern, lean face of his mother, red from the heat of the kitchen stove, and at her red arms, bare to the elbow. It was stifling in the kitchen ; something was smoking and spluttering on the stove ; there was a bitter smell and a smell of burning. The door on to the outer stairway was open. Grishka stood at the door, then, seeing his mother busy at the stove and taking no notice of him, he went out on to the staircase. It was only then, when he felt the hard dirty pavement of the landing under his feet, that he noticed that his head was aching and giddy; he felt faint, his body was overcome by a feverish lassitude.

"How stuffy it was in the kitchen," he thought.

He looked about him in a kind of perplexity, at the grey stone steps of the staircase, worn and dirty, running upwards and downwards from the narrow landing on which he stood. Opposite their door on the other side of the landing was another door, and from behind it came the sounds of two women's shrill voices; some one was scolding another. The words rained out like drops of lead from a carelessly unscrewn hanging lamp, and it seemed to Grishka that they must be running about on the dry kitchen floor and making a noise, knocking themselves against the iron and the stove. There were many words, but they all ran into one another in a shrieking hubbub of scolding words. Grishka laughed mirthlessly. He knew the people in that flat were always quarrelling, and that they often beat their naughty, dirty little children.

WHO ART THOU?

There was a window on the landing like the one in the kitchen, and from it one could look out on to the same crowded, uninteresting world—the red roofs, the yellow walls, the dusty yard. Everything was strange, foreign, unnecessary—quite unlike the sweet intimate figures of his dreams.

Grishka climbed up on to the worn slab of the window-seat, and leaned his back up against one of the wide-open frames, but he did not look out into the yard. A brightly decorated palace showed itself to his gaze; he saw in front of him a door leading to the apartment of the auburn-haired Princess Turandina. The door was opened wide, and the princess herself, seated before a high narrow window, weaving fine linen, looked round at the sound of the opening door, and stopping with her shapely white hand the noisily humming spinning-wheel, looked at him with a tender smile, saying:

"Come nearer to me, dear boy. I have waited a long time for you. Don't be afraid, come along."

Grishka went up to her and knelt at her feet, and she asked him:

"Do you know who I am?"

Grishka was charmed by the golden tones of her voice, and he answered:

THE SWEET-SCENTED NAME

" Yes, I know who you are. You are the most beautiful Princess Turandina, daughter of the mighty king of this land, Turandon."

The princess smiled gaily and said to him :

" Yes, you know that, but you don't know all. I learnt from my father, the wise King Turandon, how to weave spells and enchantments, and I am able to do with you as I will. I wanted to have a little game with you, and so I cast a spell over you and you went away from your princely home and from your father, and now, you see, you have forgotten your real name, and you have become the child of a cook, and you are called by the name of Grishka. You have forgotten who you are, and you can't remember until I choose that you should."

" Who am I ? " asked Grishka.

Turandina laughed. An evil light gleamed in her cornflower-blue eyes like the light in the eyes of a young witch not yet accustomed to the art of sorcery. Her long fingers pressed hard against the boy's thin shoulder. She teased him, speaking like a little street-girl :

" Shan't tell you. Shan't tell you for

anything. Guess yourself. Shan't tell you, shan't. If you don't guess yourself you'll always be called Grishka. Listen, there's your mother the cook calling you. Go along and be obedient to her. Go quickly or she'll beat you."

III

Grishka listened; he heard his mother's harsh voice calling from the kitchen :

" Grishka, Grishka, where are you ? you bad boy, where have you hidden yourself ? "

Grishka jumped quickly down from the window-seat and ran into the kitchen. He knew when his mother called like that he mustn't dawdle, he must go at once. And all the more just now when his mother was busy preparing dinner. She was always angry then, and especially when the kitchen was hot and stuffy. The bright apartment of the Princess Turandina faded from his sight. The blue smoke of something burning on the kitchen stove floated out to him. He was again conscious that his head ached and swam ; he at once felt tired and languid.

His mother called out to him :

" Now look lively ; run along quickly to Milligan's and buy half a pound of lemon biscuits and a shillingsworth of cakes. Hurry up, I've just got to take in tea; the mistress has some visitors—some devil has brought them here at this outlandish hour."

Grishka ran off into the corridor to find his shoes and stockings, but Anushka cried after him angrily :

" What are you doing there ? There's no time to get your shoes—go as you are. You must run there and back in no time."

Grishka took the money, a silver rouble, and held it tight in his burning palm. Then he put on his hat and ran off down the staircase. And as he ran he thought :

" Who am I ? How can I have forgotten my real name ? "

He had a long way to go, several streets away, because the cakes his mother wanted couldn't be got in the shop opposite but only in this distant one. The mistress thought that the cakes in the shop near by were always fly-blown and not well made, but those in the other shop, where she herself made purchases, were good and clean and specially nice.

" Who am I ? " thought Grishka persistently.

All his dreams about the beautiful Princess Turandina were interrupted by this tiresome question. He ran along quickly in his bare feet on the hard pavements of the noisy streets, meeting many strangers, getting in front of strangers, among this multitude of rough, unpleasant people, all hurrying somewhere, pushing their way along and looking contemptuously at little Grishka in his blue print shirt and short little dark-blue knickers. Grishka was again conscious of the strangeness and incongruity of the fact that he, who knew so many delightful stories, and who loved to dream about fair ladies, should be living in this dull and cruel town, should have grown up in just this place, in a wretched stuffy kitchen, where everything was so strange and foreign to him.

He remembered how, a few days ago, the captain's son, Volodya, who lived in No. 24 flat, had called across from the second-floor window of the opposite block and asked him to come and have a talk. Volodya was the same age as Grishka, a lively, affectionate boy, and the two children sat down on the window-seat and chatted gaily together. Suddenly the door opened, and Volodya's mother, a sour-faced woman, appeared on the threshold. Screwing up her eyes, she scrutinised Grishka from head to foot, making him feel suddenly frightened, and then she drawled, in a contemptuous tone of voice :

" What's this, Volodya ? Why have you got this wretched little barefooted boy here ? Go off indoors, and in future don't dare to try and make his acquaintance."

Volodya got red and muttered something or other, but Grishka had already run off home to the kitchen.

Now, in the street, he thought to himself :

" It's impossible that it's all like that. I can't be really only Grishka, the cook's little boy, whom nice children like Volodya and the general's son aren't allowed to know."

And in the baker's shop, when he was buying the cakes he had been sent for— none of which would fall to his own share,— and all along his homeward way, Grishka was thinking sometimes about the beautiful Turandina, the proud and wise princess, sometimes of the strange actuality of the life around him, and he thought again :

" Who am I ? And what is my own real name ? "

He imagined that he was the son of an emperor, and that the proud palace of his forefathers stood in a beautiful far-off land. He had long been suffering from a grievous complaint, and lay in his quiet sleeping-chamber. He was lying on a soft down bed under a golden canopy, covered by a light satin counterpane, and in his delirium he imagined himself to be Grishka, the cook's little son. Through the wide open window was wafted in to the sick child the sweet scent of flowering roses, the voices of his beloved nightingales, and the splash of a pearly fountain. His mother, the Empress, sat at the head of his bed, and wept as she caressed her child. Her eyes were gentle and full of sorrow, her hands were soft, for she never washed the clothes or prepared the dinner or did sewing. When this dear mother of his worked with her fingers she only embroidered in coloured silks on golden canvas for satin cushions, and from under her delicate fingers there grew crimson roses, white lilies, and peacocks with long eye-laden tails. She was weeping now because her son lay ill, and because when at times he opened his fever-dimmed eyes he spoke strange words in an unintelligible language.

But the day would come when the little prince would recover his health and would rise from his royal bed and would remember who he was and what was his real name, and then he would laugh at his delirious fancies.

IV

Grishka felt more joyful when this thought came into his mind. He ran along more quickly, noticing nothing around him. But suddenly an unexpected shock brought him to his senses. He felt frightened, even before he understood what had taken place.

The bag containing the cakes and biscuits fell from his hand, the thin paper burst, and the yellow lemon biscuits were scattered over the worn and dirty grey pavement.

" You horrid little boy, how dare you knock into me ! " cried the shrill voice of a tall stout lady against whom Grishka had run.

She smelt unpleasantly of scent, and she held up to her small angry eyes a horrible tortoiseshell lorgnette. Her whole face looked rude and angry and repulsive, and Grishka was filled with terror and distress. He looked up at her in fright, and did not know what to do. He thought that perhaps dvorniks and policemen, dreadful fantastic beings, would come from all directions and seize him and drag him away somewhere.

By the side of the lady stood a young

man, very much overdressed, wearing a top hat and horrible yellow gloves. He looked down upon Grishka with his fierce protruding reddish eyes, and everything about him looked red and angry.

" Good - for - nothing little hooligan," he hissed through his teeth.

With a careless movement he knocked off the child's cap from his head, gave him a box on the ear, and turning again to the lady, said :

" Come along, mamma. It's not worth having anything more to do with such a creature."

" But what a rude and daring boy he is," said the lady, turning away. " Dirty little ragamuffin, where were you pushing yourself ? You've quite upset me. Fancy not being able to walk quietly along the streets. What can the policemen be doing ? "

The lady and her companion, talking angrily to one another, walked away. Grishka picked up his cap and collected as many as he could of the scattered cakes and biscuits, putting them into the torn paper bag, and ran off home. He felt ashamed and he wanted to weep, but no tears came. He could no longer dream about Turandina, and he thought :

" She's just as bad as everybody here. She cast me into a terrible dream, and I shall never wake out of that dream, and for ever I shall be unable to remember my real name. And I shall never be able to answer truly the question, ' Who am I ? ' "

Who am I, sent into this world by an unknown will for an unknown end ? If I am a slave, then whence have I the power to judge and to condemn, and whence come my lofty desires ? If I am more than a slave, then why does all the world around me lie in wickedness, ugliness, and falsehood ?

Who am I ?

The cruel but still beautiful Turandina laughs at poor Grishka, at his dreams and his vain questionings.

The Dress of the Lily and of the Cabbage

IN a flower-bed in a garden grew a lily. She was all white and red—proud and beautiful.

She spoke gently to the wind passing over her. " Be more careful," said she. " I am a royal lily, and even Solomon, the wisest of men, was not clothed so luxuriously and so beautifully as I."

Not far away, in the kitchen garden, a cabbage was growing.

She heard the lily's words, and she laughed and said :

" That old Solomon, in my opinion, was just a *sans-culotte*. How did they clothe themselves, these ancients ? They cut out somehow or other a garment to cover their nakedness, and they imagined that they were arrayed in the very best fashion. But *I* taught people how to dress themselves, and the credit ought to be given to me.

" You take a bare cabbage-stalk and you

put on it the first covering, an under-vest ; over that something to fasten it ; then an under-skirt and fastenings for it ; over this you put a skirt and its fastenings, and then a buckle. After the buckle you put on another vest and skirt and fastenings and bodice and buckle. Then you cover it all up from the sides, over the top and up from the bottom, so that the cabbage - stalk is quite hidden. And then it's quite warm and decent."

She who wore a Crown

IT was a very ordinary, poorly furnished room in St. Petersburg. Elèna Nikolàevna stood at the window and looked out into the street.

There was nothing interesting to look at in the noisy and somewhat dirty town street, but Elèna Nikolàevna did not look out because she wanted to look at anything interesting. True, it would soon be time for her little son to come round the corner on his way home from school, but Elèna Nikolàevna would not have gone to the window just for that. She had such confident pride in him and in herself. He would come at the right time, as he always did—as everything in life would come at its own appointed time.

Standing there, erect and proudly confident, there was an expression on her beautiful pale face as if she wore a crown.

She was remembering something which had happened ten years ago, in that year when her husband had died, leaving her so soon after their wedded life had begun.

How terrible his death had been ! One fine spring morning he had gone out of the house quite well and happy, and before evening he had been brought home dead— run over on the highway. It had seemed then to Elèna Nikolàevna that life could never more bring her happiness. She might have died from grief, but the fingers of her little child drew her back to life, and in the old dreams of her childhood she was able to find consolation. Yet how difficult it had been to live ; how poor she had been !

The summer after her husband's death she had spent in the country with her younger sister and her own little child. And to-day she remembered with a marvellous distinctness one bright day on which had happened something delightful and strange—something apparently insignificant in itself, yet shedding upon her soul a wonderful light, illuminating all the rest of her life. On that wonderful day, long past, had happened that which ever afterwards made Elèna Nikolàevna as proudly calm as if she had been crowned queen of a great and glorious land.

But this well-remembered day had dawned

in the darkness of grief, and like every day of that summer it had been watered by her tears.

She had quickly accomplished the little household duties that were necessary and had gone into the forest so as to be far away from everybody. She loved to wander in the depths of the forest and dream there. Often she wept there, remembering the happiness that had been hers.

There was one glade which she especially loved. The soft moist grass, the clear far-away sky, the northern moistness, the tender mossy slopes, the soft clouds—all were in sympathy with her grief.

She stood by a grey boulder in this favourite spot; her clear blue eyes gazed at the scene; in her dreams she was far away. She thought she heard herself called, that a voice said:

" Elèna, what are you dreaming about ? "

She trembled, and in a moment her sweet dream lost itself in a maze of fancies—she could not have told her dream.

And why should she tell any one what her thoughts had been, where they had wandered ? No one else could understand . . . those dreamland princesses clothed in shining garments, clear-eyed, celestial . . .

who came and comforted her . . . what meaning had they for others ?

She stood alone in the quiet glade, her hands crossed upon her breast. Her blue eyes were shadowed by grief. The sun, shining high above her, caressed her back and shoulders, his rays gleaming on her long red plaits of hair encircled her with a golden halo. She dreamed. . . . Suddenly she heard voices and laughter.

Before her stood three shining maidens, three woodland princesses. Their dresses were white, as Elèna's own, their eyes were blue like hers. On their heads were fragrant flower-crowns. Their arms were bare as were Elèna's, their shoulders were kissed by the sun like hers. Their little slightly sunbrowned feet, like hers, were bathed in the dew of the grass.

They came towards her and smiled, and said :

" How beautiful she is ! "

" She stands there and the sunlight makes her hair look golden."

" She holds herself like a queen."

Joy and grief were strangely mingled in Elèna's heart. Holding out her hands in welcome she spoke joyously in her ringing voice :

SHE WHO WORE A CROWN

" Greeting, dear sisters, dear woodland princesses ! "

Clearly, clearly, like a little golden bell, sounded the voice of Elèna, and clear as the ringing of golden bells came in answer the gentle laughter of the three as they said :

" We are princesses—who art thou ? "

" Thou should'st be the queen of this place."

Sadness tinged Elèna's voice as she answered :

" How could I be a queen ? No crown of gold is mine ; my heart is full of sadness for the loss of my beloved. No one can crown me more."

The sisters smiled no longer. Elèna heard the quiet voice of the eldest sister :

" Why this earthly grief ? Thy beloved is dead, but is he not ever with thee ? Thy heart is sad, but in the remembrance of him canst thou not rejoice ? Canst thou not raise thy desires to flow in union with the Heavenly Will ? Dost thou not desire to be crowned here as our queen ? "

" Ah, I do desire it," cried Elèna, and she trembled with joy and shining tears sparkled in her blue eyes.

Once more a question came :

" And wilt thou then be worthy of thy crown ? "

Awe and wonder held the soul of Elèna, and she said :

" I will be worthy of my crown."

Then the princess spoke again :

" Stand always in the presence of fate as pure and brave as now thou standest here before us. Look straight into the eyes of men. Triumph over grief ; fear neither life nor the approach of death. Drive far from thee all mean desires and slavish thoughts. In poverty and in bondage and in misery let thy soul be proud and free."

Tremblingly she answered :

" Though in slavery, I will be free."

" Then you shall wear a crown," said the princesses.

" Yes, you shall wear a crown," said they.

They plucked the white and yellow blossoms ; with their white hands they wove a chaplet of flowers — the fragrant flower-crown of the woodland nymphs.

Thus Elèna was crowned, and the nymphs joining hands danced about her in a gentle dance — with joyful motion they encircled her.

Fast and faster — the white dresses floated

in the air, the light dancing feet moved over the dew-laden grass.

Encircling, enclosing, they drew her into their swift circle of ecstasy — away from grief, from the sadness and anxiety of life, they drew her away with them.

Time fulfilled itself, and the day waned, and grief was as a flame of joy; the soul of Elèna lost itself in rapture.

Then they kissed her and departed.

" Farewell, dear queen of ours ! "

" Farewell, dear sisters ! "

Among the trees they disappeared; Elèna was alone.

Proudly she walked upon her homeward way; she wore her crown of flowers.

She told no one of her adventure in the forest, but so radiant was her face that her little sister smiled at her and said :

" Elèna looks a shining one to-day; one might think it was the day of her angel."

In the evening Elèna went to visit little Paul, a sick child, who had not long to live. She loved the boy because he was peaceful and serene and nothing disturbed the calmness of his mind. Sometimes at night she would wake and remember little Paul and weep because he must die so soon—and the grief in her heart was strangely mingled :

for her husband who was dead, for herself so early left forlorn, for the child who so soon must die.

Paul was sitting by himself in a summer-house on the cliff watching the peaceful flaming of the setting sun. He smiled at Elèna's approach ; her coming was always a joy to him. He loved her because she always told him the truth and never sought to comfort him with false hopes as did others. He knew that he must die soon and that there were only two who would long remember him — his mother and his friend Elèna.

Elèna told him what had happened in the forest, and little Paul closed his eyes and sat in thought. But by and by he spoke and said, smiling happily :

" I am glad for you, my dear forest queen. I have always known that you were pure and free. Every one who can speak of himself and say, ' I,' ought to be as a conqueror upon the earth. For man can overcome the world."

Then he saw three young ladies walking below the cliff, and said to Elèna :

" Look ! your three woodland princesses are coming by."

Elèna looked also, and she recognised

them with a momentary feeling of pain. Three ordinary girls ! They wore the same white dresses as in the morning ; their eyes were as blue, their hair as golden, their figures as beautiful—but now they wore no flower crowns, but instead white summer hats. They were just ordinary young girls —summer visitors.

They were hidden for a moment behind the bushes, but soon they appeared again, climbing up the cliff and coming along the narrow path which passed the summer-house. Paul bowed to them and smiled, and they recognised Elèna.

" Greeting to you, dear queen."

" Dear sisters," said Elèna happily.

.   .   .   .   .   .

And ever since that time Elèna had known joy. Under the guise of the ordinary she had known the joy of her crowned life. All poverty and wretchedness had been transformed by her queenly pride, her exalted dignity.

And now after many years, as she stood by the window waiting for her little son, though her dress was poor and shabby, she was whispering to herself as she remembered the crowning day of her life :

" Man can overcome the world."

The Delicate Child

THERE once lived a delicate child.

When he was born they put him in a glass bell-jar, so that flies should not torment him.

So he lived in the bell-jar.

The boy looked out through the glass and saw the birch tree shaking in the wind. But he did not know that it was from the wind, the delicate boy did not know.

And he cried out to the birch tree :

" Don't shake, stupid birch, you'll break yourself."

The wind ceased to blow and the birch became still. And the delicate boy was very pleased, and so cried out :

" That's a sensible tree, I'm glad you listened to me."

The Bit of Candy

A LITTLE girl had some candy in a piece of paper.

At first there was much candy, but she ate it till there was only one lump left.

And she asked herself should she eat this lump also or should she give it to the poor.

" I'll give it to a poor girl," said she.

But after a while she thought : " Perhaps it would be better to divide the candy in half and share it." So she ate up half the lump.

Then she thought about the bit that was left, and she said to herself : " I'll break that in two again and give half of it to the little girl."

At last so little remained of the lump of candy that it wasn't worth while giving it to the poor girl—so she ate up what was left.

The Lump of Sugar

THERE was once a landlady. She had a little key to unlock a little cupboard. In the little cupboard was a little box, and in the little box was a wee wee lump of sugar.

And the landlady had a little doggie, and the doggie was very capricious and liked to catch hold of the end of the landlady's skirt and tug at it.

The landlady took her little key and opened the little cupboard, found the little box and took out the wee wee lump of sugar. The little doggie looked up at her and wagged his tail.

But the landlady said :

" You tugged at my skirt, Capriza Petrovna, so see this little lump of sugar, well, you shan't have it."

And she put the sugar back where it was before. The little doggie repented, yes, but it was too late.

The Bull

A LITTLE boy had a mama who wore light blue spectacles and a papa who wore dark blue ones.

They weighed in a pair of scales all that the little boy ate, meat, bread, milk, weighed it all.

At last, one day, papa said to mama :

" Our boy has to-day finished his first bull, to-morrow he starts on his second."

When the little boy heard this he began to cry, and he said :

" I don't want to eat a bull—a bull has got horns."

The Golden Post

BOBBY was angry with his papa and said to his nurse :

"As soon as I grow up I'll get to be a general, and I'll come to papa's house with a cannon and take him prisoner and tie him up to a post."

Papa, overhearing, cried out :

"Ah, you bad boy ! Tie papa to a post, would you ? That would hurt papa badly."

Bobby took fright, and said hesitatingly :

"But, papa, you know it would be a golden post, with a bit of writing on it—
'For Bravery.' "

So Arose a Misunderstanding

A BOY once asked :
    " What is coming ? "
    " I don't know," said his mother.
" But I know," said the boy.
" What ? " asked the mother.
The boy laughed and answered :
" I shan't say."
Mother got angry, complained to papa. Papa cried out :
    " What are you laughing about ? "
    " What ? " said the little boy.
    " Insulting your mother ! What do you know ? "
The boy went pale and answered :
    " I don't know anything. I was joking."
Papa got more and more angry. He thought the boy knew something, so he bellowed at him in a dreadful voice :
    " Say out what you know ! Say what is coming ! "
The boy began to cry and could not say what was coming.
In that way arose a misunderstanding.

Frogs

TWO frogs met, one a little older, the other a little younger. Said the older : "Can you croak in other ways ? "

"Rather," said the younger, "I should think I could."

"Then go ahead," said the elder.

The younger frog then began to croak in this way :

"Kva . . . kva-kva . . . " and tried various tones, but the elder cried out :

"Oh, ho, you're only croaking Russian just the same."

"How else should I croak ? " asked the younger.

"Well in French for instance," replied the elder.

"No one croaks in French," said the younger.

"Yes they do," said the elder.

"Then you do it," said the younger.

"Kvew, kvew, kvew," said the elder.

FROGS

" I can do that," said the younger.

" Go ahead, then," said the elder.

" Kvee, kvee, kvee," said the younger one, trying.

But the elder one laughed and cried out : " That sounds more like German than French, you with your *kvee*."

The younger one tried hard but couldn't make *kvew*. Cried a little and then said :

" Russian frogs croak better than French ones—more clearly."

The Lady in Fetters

IN the house of a certain Moscow physician there is a magnificent picture gallery, which after the death of its owner will become the property of the town, though now it is little known and difficult to get at. In this gallery hangs a picture, strange in its conception but marvellously painted, not at all well known, though it is the work of a highly-gifted Russian artist. In the catalogue this picture is designated by the title, " A Legend of the White Night."

The picture is of a young lady dressed in an exquisitely simple black gown, and wearing a broad-brimmed black hat with a white feather. She is seated on a bench in a garden just budding into Spring. Her face is very beautiful, but it holds an enigmatical expression. In the unreal and enchanting light of the white night which the artist has so marvellously represented it seems at times that the lady is smiling in joy, and at times the same smile seems to

106

possess a haggard expression of terror and despair.

Her hands are not seen—they are folded behind her back, and from the pose of her shoulders one feels that her arms are bound. Her feet are bare and very beautiful. They are encircled with gold bracelets and fastened together by a short gold chain. The contrast of the black dress and white naked feet is beautiful yet strange.

The picture was painted some years ago by the young artist Andrew Pavlovitch Kragaef, after a strange white night spent by him with the lady of the picture—Irene Vladimirovna Omejina—in her country villa outside Petersburg.

It was at the end of May. The day had been warm and enchantingly clear. In the morning, or rather about the time when the working - folk are going to their dinner, Kragaef was called up on the telephone. A well-known woman's voice said :

" It's I—Madame Omejina. Are you disengaged to - night, Andrew Pavlovitch ? I shall expect you here punctually at two o'clock."

" Thank you, Irene Vladimirovna——" began Kragaef.

But the lady interrupted him.

"That's right. I shall expect you. Exactly at two."

And she hung up the receiver. Her voice sounded unusually cold and unmoved—the voice of some one preparing for some significant action. This and the brief conversation made Kragaef wonder not a little. He was accustomed to have long talks on the telephone, and with a lady the conversation often went on quite a while. Irene Vladimirovna had been no exception to this, and her brevity was something new and unexpected—the young man's curiosity was aroused.

He resolved to be most punctual and to get there at two o'clock precisely. He ordered a motor in good time to take him there—he hadn't one of his own.

Kragaef was fairly well acquainted with Madame Omejina, though not intimate with her. She was the widow of a rich landowner who had died some years before. She had her own estates, and the villa to which she had invited Kragaef that evening belonged to her.

There had been strange rumours about her married life. It had been said that her husband often beat her cruelly. And people often wondered that she, an independent woman, should endure this and not leave him. There were no children, and people thought it strange that they went on living together.

It was exactly two o'clock by Kragaef's watch, and already quite light when the automobile slowed up at the entrance to the familiar villa. Kragaef had been there several times during the previous summer. On this occasion, however, he felt a curious perturbation.

" I wonder if there will be any one else, or if I'm the only visitor," thought he. " It would be more pleasant to be alone with her on such a beautiful night."

No other carriage was to be seen at the gates. Everything was quiet in the dark garden, and there were no lights to be seen in the windows.

" Shall I wait ? " asked the chauffeur.

" No, it's not necessary," said Kragaef, as he paid and dismissed him.

The side gate was open a little way. Kragaef went in and shut it after him. He glanced at the gate and saw the key in it, and impelled by some undefined presentiment, he turned the key in the lock.

He walked quietly up the gravel-path to the house. There was a cool air from the river; somewhere in the bushes the first birds of the morning twittered faintly and uncertainly.

Suddenly a familiar voice called out to him—the voice he had heard on the telephone —that strangely cold and indifferent voice.

" I'm here, Andrew Pavlovitch," said Mme Omejina.

Kragaef turned in the direction of the voice and saw his hostess seated on a bench near a flower-bed.

She sat there and looked up at him smiling. She was dressed exactly as he afterwards painted her in the picture; in the same black gown of an exquisitely simple cut, entirely without any ornament or trimming—in the same black broad-brimmed hat with a white feather—her hands were clasped behind her back and seemed to be fastened there—there, calmly resting on the gravel - path were her bare white feet encircled by golden bracelets—the thin gold chain which fastened them just glittering in the half-light.

She was smiling just that same uncertain smile which Kragaef afterwards showed in her portrait, and she said to him :

" Good evening, Andrew Pavlovitch. I felt sure somehow that you would not fail

to come at the appointed time. Pardon me
for not giving you my hand—my arms are
fastened behind me."

Then, seeing his movement towards her,
she laughed constrainedly and said :

" No, no, don't be alarmed ! You needn't
unfasten me. It's all necessary—it's what
he wishes. His night has come once more.
Sit down here beside me."

" Whom do you mean ? " asked Kragaef,
sitting down beside her and speaking cautiously and in wonder.

" My husband," answered she quietly.
" To-day is the anniversary of his death. He
died just at this hour, and every year on this
night and at this moment I give myself up
to his power. Every year he chooses some
one into whom he sends his spirit, and he
comes to me and tortures me for hours. He
cannot be restrained. He goes away, and
I am free till the following year. This time
he has chosen you. But I can see that you
are astounded—you are ready to think that
I am mad."

" Pardon me, Irene Vladimirovna," Kragaef was beginning to say.

The lady stopped him with a slight movement of her head, and said :

" No, I'm not out of my mind. Listen !

I'll tell you all about it, and you will understand me. It's not possible that such a sensitive and responsive person as yourself —such a wonderful and delicate artist— should not understand."

Now, when a man is appealed to as a sensitive and delicate person, of course he is prepared to understand all that is wanted. And Kragaef began to feel himself in sympathy with the spiritual condition of the lady. He wanted to kiss her hand in token of his sympathy, and he thought with pleasure of raising her small delicate hand to his lips. But this he could not do—he contented himself with gently squeezing her elbow in his hand.

The lady responded by an inclination of her head. Smiling uncertainly and strangely, so that it was impossible to know whether it were for happiness or a desire to weep, she said :

" My husband was a weak and a wicked man. I cannot understand even now why I loved him and couldn't leave him.

" He tortured me—at first timidly, but every year more openly and cruelly. He inflicted all kinds of torture on me, and he soon discovered a very simple and ordinary way. I can't think why I put up with it.

THE LADY IN FETTERS

Perhaps I expected something from it—but, however it may be, I became weak and wicked before him, as a humble slave."

And then she calmly began to tell in detail how her husband had treated her. She spoke as if it were of some one other than herself who had endured all his cruelty and mockery.

Kragaef listened with pity and indignation, but her voice sounded so unmoved, and there was so much evil contagion in her words, that he suddenly began to feel within himself a wild desire to throw her on to the ground and beat her as her husband had done. The longer she talked and the more she described in detail how her husband had treated her, the stronger became his feeling and the greater his desire. At first it seemed to him that his anger at the shameless frankness with which she told of her sufferings, with her quiet, almost innocent cynicism, aroused this wild desire in him. But soon he understood that there was a much deeper reason for this wicked feeling.

Was it not, in truth, the soul of the dead husband becoming incarnate in himself, the monstrous spirit of an evil, weak torturer ? He was terrified at first, but soon this momentary pang of terror died away in his soul, and more powerfully there arose in him the lust for torture—the evil and mean infection.

" I endured all this," continued the lady, " and never once did I complain. Even my spirit was unmurmuring. But one day in Spring-time I became just as weak as he. A strong desire arose in me that he should die. Perhaps his cruelty was greater just then, or it may be that the beautiful white nights of Spring acted upon me in this way. I don't know how the desire arose within me. So strange it was ! I had never before been weak or wicked. Some days I struggled with the shameful wish. I sat at the window at night, and looked out at the quiet twilight of the night of our northern city, and in grief and anger I pressed my hands together and thought with insistent evil force, 'Die, cursed one, die ! ' And it happened that he did die suddenly, on this very day, exactly at two o'clock. But I didn't kill him—oh, don't think it was I who killed him."

" Mercy on us, I don't think it ! " said Kragaef, though his voice sounded almost angry.

" He died of his own accord," continued she. " Or perhaps it was the force of my will that sent him to his grave. Perhaps the will of man is sometimes as strong as that, eh? I don't know. But I did not feel repentant. My conscience was clear. And I lived calmly on until the next Spring. But then my mind grew disturbed, and the clearer became the nights the worse it was with me. My distress increased more and more. At last, on the anniversary of his death, he suddenly came to me and spent many hours torturing me as he had done in life."

"Ah-ha, he came!" said Kragaef, with sudden malice.

"Of course you understand," said Mme Omejina, "that it was not the deceased come from his grave. He was too well brought up and too much of a townsman for such a fraud as that. He knew how to arrange it differently. He took possession of the will and spirit of a man who, like yourself, came to me that night and tortured me long and cruelly. And when he went away and left me powerless from suffering, I wept as if I had been a ruined girl. But my soul was calm, and I did not think of him again until the following year. But every year when the white nights come on I am tormented with distress, and on the night of his death my torturer comes to me."

"Every year?" asked Kragaef, his voice hoarse with malice or agitation.

"Every year," said she, "somebody comes to me at this time, and every year it is as if the actual soul of my husband rejoiced in my accidental tormentor. Then, after my dreadful night, my anguish leaves me and I can live again in the world. It happens so every year. This year he wanted you to come to me. He desired me to wait for you here in this garden, dressed as I am, barefoot and with my hands bound. And I have obeyed his will, and I sit here and wait."

She looked at Kragaef, and on her face was that blending of expression which he afterwards represented with such art in the picture.

He got up with a somewhat unnecessary haste; his face had become very pale. He felt in himself an evil passion, and seizing the lady by the shoulder he cried out to her in a hoarse voice which he could not recognise as his own:

"It's been like this every year, and this year will be no different from the others. Come!"

She stood up and began to weep. Kragaef, still grasping her by the shoulder, drew her towards the house, and she followed him, trembling with cold and the dampness of the gravel path under her bare feet, hastening and stumbling, feeling at each step the painful restraint of her golden chain, and making her golden anklets jangle—so they passed into the house.

The Kiss of the Unborn

I

A PERT little boy in buttons put his close-cropped head in at the door of a room where five lady-typists were clattering on their machines, and said :

" Nadezhda Alexevna, Mrs. Kolimstcheva is asking for you on the telephone."

A tall well-built girl of twenty-seven got up and went downstairs to the telephone. She walked with quiet self-possession, and had that deep steadfastness of gaze only given to those who have outlived heavy sorrows and patiently endured them to the end.   She was thinking to herself :

" What has happened now ? "

She knew already that if her sister wanted to speak to her it was because something unpleasant had occurred—the children were ill, the husband worried over business, they were in need of money—something of that sort.   She would have to go there and see what could be done—to help, to sympathise,

118

to put matters right. Her sister was ten years older than herself, and as she lived in a remote suburb they rarely met.

She went into the tiny telephone - box, smelling of tobacco, beer, and mice, took up the speaking-tube, and said :

" Yes. Is it you, Tanichka ? "

The voice of her sister, tearful, agitated, exactly as she had expected to hear it, answered her :

" Nadia, for God's sake come here quickly ! Something dreadful has happened. Serezha is dead. He's shot himself."

Nadezhda Alexevna could hardly realise the news. Her little nephew was dead— dear little Serezha, only fifteen years old. She spoke hurriedly and incoherently :

" *What* is it, Tanya ? How terrible ! Why did he do it ? When did it happen ? "

And neither hearing nor waiting for answer, she added quickly :

" I'll come at once, at once."

She put down the speaking-tube, forgetting even to hang it up in its place again, and hurried away to ask the manager for leave of absence.

It was given her, though unwillingly. " You know we have a specially busy time just now, before the holidays," grumbled the manager. " You always seem to want leave at the most awkward moment. You can go if it's really necessary, but don't forget that your work must be made up."

II

A few minutes later Nadezhda Alexevna got into a tram-car and began her twenty minutes' journey. She felt depressed and uncertain. Spasms of keen pity for her sister and regret for the dead boy caught at her heart.

It was terrible to think that this fifteen-year - old child, but lately a light - hearted schoolboy, should have suddenly shot himself —painful to imagine the mother's grief. How she would weep—her life seemed always to have been unhappy and unsuccessful.

Yet Nadezhda Alexevna could not give herself up entirely to such thoughts. Her mind was dwelling on something else. It was always so with her when she came to one of those times common enough in this life of unexpected happenings—the interruption of the ordinary daily routine by some unpleasant occurrence. There was an event in the background of her own life which weighed her down with a continuous and gnawing sorrow. For her there could be no relief in tears, they seemed to have been stopped at their source; rare indeed was it for a few miserable drops to force themselves to her eyes. She generally looked out upon the world with an expression of dull indifference.

So now, once again, memory revolved before her that passionate flaming circle of her past life. She recalled once more that short time of love and self-forgetfulness, of passion and of self-abandonment.

Those bright summer days had been a festival. The blue heaven had outspread itself joyously for her delight, the summer rain had pattered down for her amusement. For her the pine odours had been more intoxicatingly sweet than roses. Roses would not grow in such a climate. Yet it was a place that the heart loved. The greeny-grey moss in the dark forest was a soft and tender couch; the forest rivulets flowing over the tumbled boulders lisped clear and sweet as streams of Arcady; their coolness gladdened and refreshed.

How quickly had the days passed in the glad rapture of love! The last day dawned, which she knew not then to be the last. The sky was cloudless, the heavens clear.

Simple happiness was all around. The broad shadowy glades of the scented pine-forest were cool and dreamy, the tender moss underfoot was soft and warm. All was as it had been on other days. Only the birds had ceased to sing—they had nested and flown away with their little ones.

But there had been a shadow on the countenance of her beloved—he had received an unpleasant letter that morning.

As he himself said :

" A dreadfully unpleasant letter. I am desperate. So many days before I see you again ! "

" How is that ? " she had said. Sadness had not yet touched her.

" My father writes to say that my mother is ill and that I ought to go home."

His father had written something quite different—but Nadezhda Alexevna did not know that. She had not yet learnt that it is possible to be deceived in love, that the lips that kiss may speak lies instead of truth.

With his arms around her and his lips kissing hers he had said :

" I must go, there's nothing else to do. How lonely I shall be ! I can't think anything serious is the matter, but I shall be obliged to go."

THE KISS OF THE UNBORN

" Why, of course," said she. " If your mother is ill, how could you stay ! Write to me every day ; it will be so dull when you are gone."

She went with him as usual as far as the high road, and then home again along the forest path, sad at his departure, yet certain of his return. And he had never come back.

She had received two or three letters from him, strange letters, confused, full of half-expressed feelings, hints of something she could not understand. Then no more. Nadezhda Alexevna began to realise that he had ceased to love her. And when the summer had come to an end she heard a chance conversation which told her of his marriage.

" Why, haven't you heard ? Last week. They went off to Nice for the honeymoon."

" Yes, he's fortunate. He's married a rich and beautiful girl."

" She has a large dowry, I suppose."

" Yes, indeed. Her father . . ."

Nadezhda Alexevna did not stay to hear about the father. She moved away.

She often remembered all that had happened afterwards. Not that she wished to remember—she had striven to stifle recollection and to forget the past. It had all been so grievous and humiliating, and there had seemed no way of escape. It was then, in those first dreadful days after she knew he was married to another, in those sweet places made dear to her by the memory of his kisses, that she had first felt the movements of her child—and linked with the first thoughts of a new life had come the forebodings of death. No child must ever be born to her!

No one at home had ever known—she had thought out some pretext for getting away. Somehow or other, with great difficulty, she had got enough money together and had managed everything—she never wished to remember how—and had returned to her home, weak and ill, with pallid face and tired body, yet with heroic strength of spirit to conceal her pain and terror.

Memory often tried to remind her of all that had taken place, but Nadezhda Alexevna refused to acknowledge its power. When sometimes in a flash she recalled everything, she would shudder with horror and repulsion and resolutely turn her mind away at once from the picture.

But in her heart there was one memory which she treasured; she had a child, though it had never come to birth, and she often saw before her a sweet yet terrible image of the little one.

Whenever she was alone and sitting quietly by herself, if she closed her eyes, the child came to her. She felt that she watched him grow. So vividly did she see him that at times it seemed to her that day after day and year after year she had lived with him as an actual mother with her living child. Her breasts were full of milk for him. At a sudden noise she trembled—perhaps the child had fallen and would be hurt.

Sometimes she put out her hand to stroke his soft, bright, golden curls, to touch his hand, to draw him nearer. But he always escaped her touch, her hand met empty air, and yet she heard his little laughing voice as if he were still near and hiding just behind her chair.

She knew his face—the face of her child who had never been born. It was quite clear to her—that dear yet terrible blending of the features of him who had taken her love and discarded it, who had taken her soul and drained it and forgotten, the blending of the features of him who, in spite of all, was still so dear with her own features.

His grey eyes and wavy golden hair and the soft outline of his lips and chin were all his father's. The little pinky shell-like ears, the rounded limbs, the rosy dimpled cheeks were her own.

She knew all his little body—all. And his little baby ways—how he would hold his tiny hands, how he would cross one foot over the other—learning from the father he had never seen. His smile was like her own—he had just that same trick of dropping his head on one side in blushing confusion.

Painfully sweet memories. The tender, rosy fingers of her child touched her deep wounds, and were cruel though dear. So painful! But she never wished to drive him away.

" I cannot, cannot do without thee, dear little unborn son of mine. If only thou wert really living! If only I could give thee life ! "

For it was only a dream-life ! It was for her alone. The unborn can never rejoice or weep for himself. He lives, but not for himself. In the world of the living, in the midst of people and earthly things, he doesn't exist at all. So full of life, so dear, so bright, and yet he is not.

Nadezhda Alexevna used to say to herself, " And this is my doing. Now he is small and he doesn't understand. But when he grows up he will know—he will compare himself with living children, he will want to live a real life, and then he will reproach me and I shall want to die."

She never thought how foolish were such thoughts in the light of reality. She could not imagine that the unborn child renounced by her had never been the habitation of a human soul. No—for Nadezhda Alexevna her unborn child lived, and tortured her heart with an endless grief.

To her he was as a shining one, clad in bright garments, with little white hands and feet, clear innocent eyes and pure smile. When he laughed his laugh was happy and musical. True, when she wanted to caress him he evaded her, but he never went far away, he was always hiding somewhere near. He ran away from her embraces, but all the same he often seemed to put his soft, warm little arms about her neck and press his tender lips to her cheek—at those times when she sat quietly alone and closed her eyes. But never once had he kissed her on the lips.

" When he grows up he will understand," she thought. " He will be sorry, and he will go away and never come back any more. And then I shall die."

And now as she sat in the noisy, crowded

tram-car, in the company of strangers, pushing and jostling one another, Nadezhda
Alexevna closed her eyes and remembered
her own little child. Once more she looked
into his clear eyes, once more she heard the
tender lispings of his unuttered words . . .
all the way to the end of her journey, when
the time came for her to get out of the car.

III

When the tram stopped Nadezhda Alexevna made her way along the snow-covered
streets, past the low wooden and stone
houses, past the gardens and enclosed spaces
of the remote suburb. She was alone.
Many of the other passengers had been met,
but for her there was no companion. And
she thought to herself as she walked along :
"My sin will always remain with me ;
I can never get away from it. How is it
that I go on living ? Even little Serezha is
dead."

A dull pain gnawed at her heart ; she
could not answer her own question :

"Why do I go on living ? Yet why should
I die ? "

And again she thought :

"He is always with me, my dear little

one. But he is growing up now; he is eight years old, and he must be beginning to understand. Why isn't he angry with me? Doesn't he want to be able to go and play with the other children; to ride on the frozen snow in his little sledge? Doesn't all this winter beauty attract him? I feel it all so delightful; even in spite of its illusions the world is so beautiful and so enchanting. Is it possible for him not to want to live here in reality?"

Then, as she went on and on, all alone, through the monotonous streets, she began to think of those to whom she had come: her hard-worked brother-in-law, her tired sister, the crowd of fretful children always asking for something or other, the poverty-stricken home, the lack of money. She remembered her favourite nephews and nieces—and little Serezha who had shot himself.

Who could have expected him to die? He had been so gay, so lively.

And then she remembered her talk with the boy last week. Serezha had been sad and upset then. He had been reading some incident recorded in the newspapers and had said:

" Things are bad at home, and if you take

up a newspaper you only read about horrors and shameful happenings."

She had said something which she herself did not believe, in order to divert the boy's attention. Serezha had smiled grimly and then continued :

" But, Auntie Nadia, how bad it all is ! Just think what is going on all around us. Don't you think it dreadful that one of the best of people, an old, old man, went away from his home to find a place in which to die ? It must have been because he saw more plainly than we do the horrors around us, and he couldn't endure to live any longer. So he went away and died. Terrible ! "

And after a little silence he went on :

" Auntie Nadia, I tell you just what I think, because you're always kind to me and you understand—I don't want to live at all in a world where such things happen. I know I'm just as weak as everybody else, and what is there for me to do ? Only by degrees to begin to get used to it all. Auntie, Nekrasof was right when he said, ' It is good to die young.' "

Nadezhda Alexevna remembered that she had felt anxious about the child and had had a long talk with him. It seemed as if he

were convinced at last. He had smiled
again in his old way, and had said in his usual
careless tone :

" Ah, well, we shall live, and we shall see.
Progress is still going forward, and we do
not yet understand its aim."

And now Serezha no longer lived—he had
killed himself. So he hadn't wanted to live
and look on at the majestic march of Progress.
And what was his mother doing just now ?
Perhaps kissing his little waxen hand, or
perhaps getting supper for the hungry little
ones who were doubtless frightened and
crying, looking pitiful in their worn-out and
untidy clothes. Perhaps she had thrown
herself down upon her bed and was weeping,
—weeping endlessly. Happy woman, happy,
if she could weep. What in this world is
sweeter than the comfort of tears !

IV

At length Nadezhda Alexevna reached
her sister's home, and went up the staircase
to the fourth floor. It was a narrow
stone staircase with very steep flights of
stairs, and she went up so quickly, almost
running, that she lost her breath, and
stopped outside the door to rest before

going in.   She breathed heavily, holding on to the balustrade with her woollen-gloved hand.

The door was covered with felt, over which oilcloth had been stretched, and on this oilcloth was a cross of narrow black strips, partly, perhaps, for ornament, partly for strength. One of the strips was half torn off and hanging down, and behind it, through a hole in the oilcloth, protruded the grey felt.   For some reason or other this suddenly seemed pitiful and painful to Nadezhda Alexevna.   Her shoulders heaved quickly.   Covering her face with her hands she burst into loud sobbing. She felt suddenly weak, and sitting down hastily on the top step she wept.   For a long time she sat there hiding her face in her hands.   A warm rain of tears flowed over her woollen gloves.

It was nearly dark, and very cold and silent on the staircase—the doors on the landing stood dumb and rigid.   Long, long she wept. . . . Then suddenly she heard a light, familiar step, and as she waited in expectation she felt her child come nearer and put his arms about her neck.   His cheek pressed close to hers, and his warm little fingers tried to push away the hands which were screening and hiding her face.

THE KISS OF THE UNBORN

He put his lips to her cheek and whispered gently:

" Why do you weep? How can you have done wrong? "

Silently she sat and listened; she dare not move or open her eyes lest the child should disappear. She let her right hand drop on to her knee, but still kept her eyes covered with the left. Gradually her weeping became less; she must not frighten the child with her woman's tears, the tears of a sinful woman.

And the child went on, kissing her cheek as he spoke, " You haven't done wrong at all."

Then he spoke again, and now his words were those of Serezha:

" I don't want to live in this world. I'm very thankful to you, mother dear."

And again:

" Indeed, dear mother, I don't want to be alive."

These words had sounded terrible in her ears when Serezha had spoken them—terrible because spoken by one who, having received from unseen Powers the living form of mankind, ought to have held as a precious treasure the life committed to his care, and not have wished to destroy it. But these same words, spoken by the child who had never been born into this world, rejoiced his mother's heart. Gently and timidly, as if afraid of frightening him by the sound of an earthly voice, she asked :

" And my dear one forgives me ? "

And heard the answer :

" You haven't done wrong at all ; yet if you want to hear me say so, ' I forgive you.' "

And suddenly her heart overflowed with a foretaste of an unlooked-for happiness. Hardly daring to hope, hardly knowing what to expect, she slowly and fearfully stretched out her hands—and felt her child on her knees, with his little hands on her shoulders, his lips pressed close to hers in a long, long kiss.

Her eyes were fast closed still, for she feared to look on that which it is not given to mankind to see, yet it seemed to her that the child's eyes looked into hers—and that he breathed a blessing upon her—and shone upon her like a Sun.

Then she felt the arms unclose, and on the staircase she heard the light patter of feet, and knew that the child was gone.

She got up, dried her tears, and rang the bell. When she went in to her sister she was full of calm and happiness, she had power to strengthen and console.

The Hungry Gleam

SERGEY MATVEITCH MOSHKIN dined very well to-day — comparatively, of course — as a man reckons who has spent a year on other people's doorsteps and stairs searching for a job. He has dined well, but all the same the hungry gleam still remains in his sorrowful dark eyes, and gives to his lean and swarthy face an expression of unwonted significance.

Moshkin spent on his dinner his last six shilling [1] note, and there rattled in his pocket only a few coppers, and in his purse a worn fourpenny bit.[2] He made a feast and made merry, though he knew that it was stupid to rejoice, premature and unfounded. But he had sought work so hard and had come to such a pass that he was ready to rejoice even at the phantom of hope.

Moshkin had lately put an advertisement in the *Novoe Vremya*. He had advertised himself as a schoolmaster with literary gifts.

[1] Three roubles.   [2] Fifteen copecks.

THE SWEET-SCENTED NAME

He had once been correspondent of a Volga newspaper. That was why he lost his last post; some one found out that he wrote malicious tit-bits for a radical paper, informed the Head of the rural council, who in turn informed the inspector of national schools. The inspector, of course, wouldn't stand it.

"We don't want such teachers," said the inspector to him in a personal interview.

And Moshkin asked:

"Then what sort do you want?"

But the inspector, avoiding an inconvenient question, replied drily:

"Good-bye, till we meet again. Hope to see you when we meet on that beautiful shore. . . ."

Moshkin also announced in his advertisement that he would like to be secretary, editor, sub-editor, or leader-writer of a newspaper, lesson-hearer for young children, tutor, pleasant companion to any one making a tour in the Crimea, handyman about a house, etc. He also declared that he had no objection to taking a post at a distance.

He waited. There arrived one post card. Strangely enough even that post card caused him to hope.

It was the morning. Moshkin was having

his tea. In came the landlady herself. Her
little black eyes twinkled as she called out
sarcastically :

" The correspondence of Sergey Matveitch
Moshkin, Esq."

And whilst he read the card she peered
at him from under the yellow triangle of
her brow and muttered :

" Letters won't pay for board and lodging.
Letters won't fill your stomach. Better go
to people and hunt for work, not strut like
a Spaniard."

He read :

" Be kind enough to call to discuss
matters from 6 to 7 P.M., 6th Line, No. 78,
lodging 57."

Without signature.

Moshkin looked spitefully at the landlady. She stood at the door, fat, stiff, and
calm like a great, staring doll. And she
looked at him with cold, malicious, steady
eyes.

Moshkin cried out :

" Basta ! "

He struck with his fist on the table,
stood up, and commenced to march up and
down the room, all the while repeating :

" Basta ! "

The landlady softly enquired :

THE SWEET-SCENTED NAME

" Will you pay, you Kazan and Astra-khan correspondent ? Eh ? Has your ugly face any conscience left ? "

Moshkin stopped before her, stretched out in front of her his empty hand, and said expressively :

" All that I have."

He didn't say a word about the last-left three-rouble note which he had in his pocket, as yet unspent. The landlady boiled over :

" I'm not the wife of an officer of hussars : money's necessary to me. How will I get seven roubles' worth of wood ? If you don't keep yourself you're just a spending machine. Dear me, a man with abilities too, a young man, and a sufficiently charming exterior. You can find some one else to put you up. But how can I ? No matter what you turn to, out flies the money. Blow—a rouble, spit—a rouble, die—a hundred and fifty."

Moshkin walked up to her and said :

" Don't alarm yourself, Prascovia Pet-rovna, this evening I shall receive a post and will settle up."

And once more he commenced his march, shuffling in his slippers.

The landlady stood grumbling for some time, and at last went out crying :

THE HUNGRY GLEAM

" I have a breast of steel. Had it been any one else in my place they'd soon have shown you the door, saying, ' Live without me, tramp the streets, I'm not your born slave.' "

She went out, and there remained in his memory her doll-like figure, puffy arms, yellow triangle of a brow over black waxy eyes, her yellow triangle of tucked-up yellow petticoat, the little triangle of her red snuffing nose. Three triangles.

All day Moshkin was hungry, gay, and wicked. He strayed aimlessly in the streets. He looked at the girls, and they all seemed to him dear, gay, ready to be loved—by the rich. He stopped before jewellers' windows, and the hungry gleam grew keener in his eyes.

He bought a newspaper. Read it on a seat in the square where the children were running and laughing, where the nurses aped the fashions, and the air was full of dust and the smell of dry leaves—and the smell of the streets and the garden mixed disagreeably and reminded him of gutta-percha. In the newspaper Moshkin was struck by the story of a man who had gone mad through hunger, and who, in his dementia, had gone into a gallery and slashed a picture about with his knife.

" That's what. Splendid ! I understand that ! "

Moshkin strode about saying to himself :

" That's what. I understand that ! "

And afterwards, as he wandered along the rich avenues or sauntered by the grand shops of the parade, passed in and out among the equipages of Petersburg lords and ladies, rubbed elbows with the rich, the fine, the perfumed, and breathed the atmosphere of all that wonderful world of luxury to which only those who have money have the entrée, he kept on repeating to himself :

" That's what. I understand that ! "

He walked up to a great, fat, idle uniformed footman and cried :

" That's what ! I understand that ! "

The footman turned a contemptuous gaze on him, but did not move or speak. Moshkin tittered cheerfully and added :

" Fine fellows the anarchists ! "

" Clear out ! " cried the footman angrily.

Moshkin moved off. Suddenly a horrible thought occurred to him. A policeman stood near, and his white gloves caught the young man's attention. He stopped in vexation, and whispered to himself :

" A bomb would suit you very well."

THE HUNGRY GLEAM

He heard the footman spit angrily behind
him, and he walked on. He walked far,
and at about six in the evening entered a
middle-class restaurant. He took a seat
at a table by the window, drank a glass of
vodka, nibbled two anchovies, ordered dinner
at one and sixpence, drank a bottle of " Iced
Chablais." After dinner he had a liqueur.
He felt giddy a bit. Some one was playing
a barrel-organ, and his head went round to
the music. He didn't take his change,
and, leaving the restaurant with a little
swagger, he tipped the doorkeeper sixpence.

He looked at his nickel watch—it was
getting on for seven. Time. Perhaps he
would be late, and they would have engaged
some one else. He strode forward agitatedly.

Things got in his way awfully :

the roads were up ;

the sleepy cabmen kept running their
cabs in front of him as he took the crossings ;

people kept blocking the road, especially
peasants and well-dressed ladies ;

when people made way for him, turning
to their right, he made way for them, turning
to his left, and collided ;

beggars kept asking him for money ;

walking itself seemed to retard him.

It is difficult to conquer space and time

when one is in a hurry. The earth itself seems to suck you in, and at each step you feel impotence and tiredness—you feel it like a rheumatism in the marrow. Thence is spite engendered and the hungry gleam grows brighter in the eyes.

Moshkin thought :

" The devil take it, eh, all the devils ! "

However, he got there at last.

Behold the road and the house, No. 78. It was a four-storey, dark-painted house with two entrances. He went in at a great yawning gate and read the list of occupiers. Flat No. 57 was not indicated. He looked round for some one to ask, but there was no one about. At last, on a little metal plate beside the dirty-white button of an electric bell, he read : " To the House-porter."

He pressed the button and went in once more to look at the list of occupiers, but even before he got to it he met the porter, a black-bearded man of insinuative appearance.

" Where is lodging 57 ? "

Moshkin asked the question carelessly, imitating that of the chief of the rural council through whom he lost his place. He knew by experience that with house-porters it is necessary to speak in a certain sort of way and not in another. Pilgrimaging from door to door and climbing up many staircases gives a man a certain varnish.

The porter asked somewhat suspiciously :

" Who is it you want to see ? "

And with simple carelessness and a gentle drawl Moshkin replied :

" I don't really know myself. I have come about an advertisement. I received a letter, but the writer is not indicated. Only the address is given. Who lives there ? "

" Miss Engelgardova," answered the porter.

" Engelgargt ? " queried Moshkin.

The porter repeated :

" Engelgardova."

Moshkin laughed.

" Russification ? "

" Helena Petrovna," answered the porter.

" An old hag ? " asked Moshkin doubtfully. The porter grinned.

" No, sir, a young lady. By the front way, please ; through the gate on the right."

" I've looked," said Moshkin. " Only the first numbers are there."

" No," said the porter. " Fifty-seven is there, at the bottom."

THE SWEET-SCENTED NAME

Moshkin asked :

" And what is her occupation. Has she some sort of business ? A school ? A publishing office ? "

" No, I never heard either of a school or a publishing office. They have private means."

At Miss Engelgardova's a very country-looking chambermaid showed the young man to the drawing-room and asked him to wait.

He waited, grew bored and tired. He surveyed the furniture. There was an accumulation of armchairs, tables, chairs, screens, sideboards, there were little tables with busts on them, lamps, knick-knacks, mirrors on the walls, pictures, lithographs, clocks, curtains on the walls, flowers. It was close, oppressive, dark. Moshkin began to walk up and down softly on the carpet. He looked with spite at the pictures and the busts.

" To the devil, eh, to all the devils ! " thought he.

But when the lady of the house came in he hid the hungry gleam and looked at her with his eyes.

She was young, tall, ruddy cheeked, and by all accounts good - looking. She walked up to him briskly and resolutely, and then rather awkwardly held out to him her strong white arm. It was bare to the elbow.

She held her hand halfway high, as if to say " Shake it or kiss, which you please." Moshkin kissed. Pressing his lips till his teeth touched her hand, he made a loud and smacking kiss. She shuddered rather, but said nothing. She walked to the sofa, pushed aside a table, sat down, pointed to an armchair for him. He sat down. She questioned :

" That was your advertisement yesterday ? "

He blurted :

" Mine."

He thought a minute and then answered more politely :

" Mi-ne."

And he felt vexed and thought again :

" To the devil, eh ! "

She inquired what he could do, where he was brought up, where he had worked ; so cautiously she approached the real question at issue that one might have thought she was waiting for something else to happen first.

At last it became clear. She wanted

some one to edit a journal. What sort of journal ? She hadn't yet decided. Some sort. A little one. She thought of buying a paper already in existence ; of the character of the paper she said nothing. He might be useful in the counting-house perhaps, but as he had written that he was a schoolmaster she had assumed he had matriculated. Could he edit with so small a qualification ? She doubted it.

However, if he understood book-keeping . . .

How to take in subscriptions . . .

Transcribe business and editorial letters . . .

Cash postal orders . . .

Correct proofs . . .

Fold the papers, pack and address them . . .

Take them to the post . . .

And so on . . .

And so on . . .

The young lady talked for half an hour, and gave a sufficiently confused impression of the various duties.

" You need several men to do all that," said Moshkin bitterly.

The young lady blushed with vexation. Lines of greed fluttered about her face.

" The journal will be a small one, a

special one. In such a little undertaking to employ several clerks would be to risk immediate extinction."

He laughed and agreed :

" Yes, yes, I suppose. Well, time won't grow heavy on my hands."

He asked :

" But how much of the day shall I be occupied ? "

" Oh, from nine in the morning—that's not late, is it ?—to seven in the evening— that won't be too early, I suppose ? Of course sometimes when there's a rush you might stay a little longer or come in on a Sunday. Of course you're free, aren't you ? "

" How much do you think to pay me ? "

" Would one pound sixteen a month be enough ? "

He reflected and laughed :

" Rather little."

" Well, I can't go any higher than two guineas."

" Very well."

In a sudden burst of rage he put his hand in his pocket, took out the key of his room, and called out calmly but most decidedly :

" Hands up ! "

" Ah," cried the young lady, and hurriedly put up her arms.

She sat on the sofa, looking very pale. She was big and strong ; he little and emaciated.

The loose sleeves of her blouse dangled on her shoulders, and her white arms stretched upward looked those of an acrobat. She was evidently capable of holding hands up for a long time.

Enjoying her confusion, Moshkin added slowly and suggestively :

" Only move ! But tremble ! "

He went up to a picture.

" How much is it worth ? " he asked.

" Twenty-two pounds without the frame," said the young lady unhappily.

He fumbled in his pocket for his pen-knife, and then jabbed a great cross into the canvas.

" Ah ! " exclaimed the girl, holding her hands up.

He went up to a marble bust.

" How much is it worth ? "

" Thirty pounds."

He knocked off its nose with his key, then an ear, then chipped the cheeks. The lady sighed softly, and it was pleasant to hear her soft sighing.

He cut up some more pictures, cut open the back of an armchair, broke some vases.

He went up to the young lady and cried :
" Get under the sofa."

She obeyed.

" Lie quietly till some one comes or you'll
get a bomb."

He went out, met no one either in the hall
or on the staircase.

At the gate the porter stood, and Moshkin
said :

" A strange lady that of yours ! "

" How ? "

" Doesn't behave very well—makes scenes.
I should go up to her now, she's feeling bad."

" I can't go till I'm called."

" Well, you know best."

He went out. The hungry gleam grew
dimmer in his eyes.

Moshkin tramped the streets a long while,
and he recounted to himself stupidly and
deliberately the events of that drawing-
room, and pictured again the torn pictures
and the lady under the sofa.

The dim water of the canal beckoned to
him. The glimmering light of the sunset
gave the surface a beautiful sadness, a
soothing like the music sometimes made by
an insane composer. Such also were the
rough flags of the pier and such the dusty
cobbles of the roadway, and such the stupid,

dirty children coming to meet him. All was locked and inimical.

But the green-gold water of the canal beckoned.

And the hungry gleam died away, died away.

So musical was the sudden splash in the water.

And there ran away, ring beyond ring, black dark rings, wallowing over and eclipsing the green-gold water of the canal.

The Little Stick

THERE is upon the earth a very wonderful little stick which will cause all things to disappear and turn your life into a dream if you touch your head with it.

If you don't like your life just take the little stick and put it to one of your temples —and suddenly all you didn't like will become a dream and you will start something quite new.

Of that sort is the wonderful little stick.

Equality

A BIG fish overtook a little one and wanted to swallow him.

The little fish squeaked out :

" It is unjust. I also want to live. All fishes are equal before the law."

The big fish answered :

" What's the matter ? I won't discuss whether we are equal, but if you don't want me to eat you, then do you please swallow me if you can—swallow me, don't be afraid, I shan't set on you."

The little fish opened his mouth and poked about trying to get the big fish in, sighed at last and said :

" You have it. Swallow me."

Adventures of a Cobble-Stone

THERE was in the town a cobbled roadway. A wheel of a passing cart loosened one of the stones. The stone said to himself, "Why should I lie here close packed with others of my kind ? I will live separately."

A boy came along and picked up the cobble-stone.

Thought the stone to himself : "I wanted to travel and I travel. I only had to wish sufficiently strongly."

The boy threw the stone at a house. Thought the stone : "I wish to fly and I fly. It's quite simple—I just willed it."

Bang went the stone against the window-glass. The glass broke and in doing so cried out :

"Oh, you scoundrel ! What are you doing ? "

But the stone replied :

"You'd have done better to get out of the way. I don't like people getting in my way. Everything arranged for my benefit—that's my motto."

The stone fell on a soft bed and thought : " I've flown a bit, and now I'll lie down for a while and rest."

A servant came and took the stone off the bed and threw it out at the window again so that it fell back on the cobbled roadway.

Then the stone cried out to his fellow-cobbles : " Brothers, good health, I've just been paying a call at one of the mansions, but I did not at all care for the aristocracy, my heart yearned for the common people, so I returned."

The Future

NO one knows what the future will bring. But there is a place where the future gleams through an azure veil of desire. This is the place where those who are as yet unborn rest in peace. There everything is joyful, peaceful, freshly cool. No grief is there, and instead of air there is diffused an atmosphere of pure joy, in which the unborn have their being.

And no one ever leaves that land unless he desires to leave it.

Once there were four souls who all wished at the same moment to be born into this world. And in the azure mist of desire our four elements were revealed to them.

And one said :

" I love the earth—it is soft and warm and firm."

And another said :

" I love water—eternally falling, cool, and translucent."

The third said :

" I love fire—gay and bright it is, and purifying."

And the fourth said :

" I love the air—stretching out so broad and high—the light breath of life."

And this is what life brought to them.

The first became a miner, and while he was at work a shaft fell and buried him in the earth.

And the second shed tears like water, and at length was drowned.

And the third perished by fire in a burning house.

And the fourth was hanged.

Poor innocent elements ! Foolish desiring ones !

Oh, why did Will lead them forth from the happy place of non-existence !

The Road and the Light

O N a long country road came people with horses and waggons, and only the stars gave them light.

The night was a long one, but their eyes were accustomed to the darkness, and they were able to distinguish all the unevennesses and windings of the road.

But the way being long it became dull for one of the men, and he said :

" Hadn't we better light lanterns so as to see the way ? Then the horses will move more quickly and we shall get to our destination sooner."

The others believed him and lighted lanterns, and not content with that, broke off branches from the trees and made torches —they even lighted bonfires, taking much trouble over the lighting of the way.

The horses stood still. " Never mind," said the men, " we shall get on quicker afterwards."

And all around them was a bright light,

and the light of the stars was darkened. Then the wayfarers saw that there was not one road only, but many side-tracks and by-paths. And each road seemed to some one the shortest road to take.

They quarrelled among themselves as to which road to take, and they separated. The morning light found them all on different ways and far from the place whither they were bound.

The Keys

A SKELETON - KEY said to her neighbour :

"I go about everywhere, but you lie still. Where have I not been, but you've always remained at home. What are you thinking about ?"

The old key did not want to answer, but she said :

"There is a strong oaken door. I lock it, and when the time comes I unlock it again."

"Well," said the skeleton - key, "but aren't there a great many doors in the world ?"

"I don't need to know about any other doors," said the key. "I can't open them."

"Can't you ? But I can open every door !"

And the skeleton-key thought to herself :

"This key is really stupid if it can only open one door." But the key said to her :

THE SWEET-SCENTED NAME

" You're a thieves' skeleton-key, but I am a true and honest door-key."

This the skeleton-key did not understand. She did not know what truth and honesty were, and she thought that the door-key was so old that she had gone out of her mind.

The Independent Leaves

SOME leaves with very strong stalks were hanging from a branch, and they found life very dull. It was very unpleasant—they could see the birds flying and the kittens running about ; even the clouds were being carried along—and they were still on the branch. They swung themselves about, trying to break off from their stalks and be free.

They said to one another :

" We can live independent lives. We are quite grown up. But here we are under guardianship, stuck fast to this old stupid branch."

They swung themselves about and at last got free. They fell to the ground and withered. Presently the gardener came and swept them away with the refuse.

The Crimson Ribbon

I

THE old professor, Edward Henriovitch Roggenfeldt, and his aged wife, Agnes Rudolfovna, had been accustomed for many years to live from May to September in the same watering-place, in Esthonia on the southern shore of the Gulf of Finland. Every year they occupied the same beautiful country villa standing in its own grounds. From the balcony of this villa they had a broad and delightful outlook over the waters of the gulf, the meadows near the sea, and the beach.

Although this watering-place was inhabited for the most part by families of Germans, professors and physicians, and bore the stupid ridiculous name of Très-joli, it was a very pleasant and convenient place in which to live. All the people who owned villas there were firmly convinced that Esthonia was the healthiest place in the world and that Très-joli was the most beautiful spot in North-West Russia. They declared that this was printed in the Encyclopaedia in which other reliable information could be found of this sort, for example, that Edgar Poe lived a degraded life, and was a lying and evil-living man.

The peasants of the place—Esthonians— were peaceful and honest and well-behaved ; no one ever heard of fights or robberies there. There was a post and telegraph office quite near, only four versts away. The postman came twice a day, and not only brought the post but collected the letters.

There were two cafés in the neighbourhood, one on the sea-shore, the other inland, near the baron's estate, with very fine gardens. Once a week there was music in the café on the shore. Not far away, also at a distance of four versts, was an Assembly Room where there was a public dance once a week, and where one could get wine and beer or have dinners or suppers. But all this was not too near—the people who lived at Très-joli could enjoy a peaceful quietude and yet not be deprived of the conveniences of civilisation. The tradesmen brought their goods to the very doors of the villas—a great convenience, which fully compensated for not living near the town markets.

THE SWEET-SCENTED NAME

The houses in Très-joli stood on a high cliff. The bank sloped down to the sea, with here and there steep ravines in which were trees and bushes and wild narcissus, but in places the cliff was bare and laminated, rejoicing the hearts of professors and students, who found there ancient Silurian remains, green and brown and yellow layers of limestone and sandstone. Along the edge of the sea stretched a broad strip of fine friable pale yellow sand, dotted here and there with large stones and some small pebbles. The rugged boulders were ornamental, the pebbles were rather a hindrance to walking, but the sand was delightful and the bathing excellent, and on the shore in front of the villas was a row of clean-looking dressing-rooms.

The water of the gulf was of many varying tints and colours, from the palest and most delicate blue in the sunshine to the gloomiest purple in dull weather. Sometimes it was perfectly calm. Then the broad waters of the gulf lay like an enormous expanse of steel along which stripes of fleeting colour streamed.

Sometimes the waves lashed noisily along the sandy shore. The long wearisome sound like the roar of a tired and hungry animal kept nervous visitors from sleeping, flurried the hysterical, and delighted the serious fifteen-year-old schoolboys. On such days they would come down to the shore and meditate upon the " accursed " questions of life and being—those questions familiar to every progressive schoolboy of that age.

The sunsets were wonderful, each evening different. Every evening the sky arrayed itself in a new way, sometimes covering itself with clouds, sometimes appearing clear and cloudless.

If there were few clouds, or none at all, the sky showed itself in an exquisite austerity of beauty as its adornment. Then the sun, solitary, weary, purple in colour, hiding itself behind pale purple veils, sank majestically down towards the hardly distinguishable line of the horizon, sinking slowly, dying away in sadness and beauty, till at length, with a last faint gleam shining for a moment in the misty bed of the far and melancholy distance, it went out like the last sigh of an expiring universe. And then came on an undisturbed serenity both in the heavens and upon the earth, and a spell of deepening shadows was cast upon the warm sand and the cold pebbles, on the dreaming trees and on the humble roofs of the villagers, gradually chilling all.

THE SWEET-SCENTED NAME

When the sunset sky was massed with dark heavy lowering clouds, and bright foam-like cloudlets were scattered like a whimsical pattern on the blue enamel of the heavens, the departing sun was attended by a magnificence of flame and colour and radiance and delicate gold-edged beams of light. The enraptured gaze did not then behold the setting sun in the majesty of its departure, for the sun appeared as only one of the heavenly marvels, and not the most beautiful of all—only a monotonously glowing disk of a uniform crimson incandescence. All the broad and beauteous West was filled with slow streams of wavering and glimmering molten many-toned liquid gold, blazing with all the yellows of amber and half-transparent topaz, flaming through the innocent blue of heaven with all the passions and crimsons of blood, trembling and unconsumed in the flames of jasper, onyx and emerald and the glowing carmine of rubies. It seemed then as if a gigantic rainbow, glowing in the heat of the heavenly furnace, suddenly tore apart its thin half-transparent veil, poured itself through and spread out along the heavens its many-coloured stream, which broke out into innumerable fires.

Sometimes in dull weather opal clouds

166

would appear in the sky, and the pale angel of death would look down upon the earth with his unswerving gaze, right into the eyes of people who cannot perceive him.

But it is impossible to describe all the sunsets, because the diversity of them is endless, endless as the diversity of human life itself.

The most pleasant feature of Très-joli was its delightful combination of sea and forest, the trees in some places coming down nearly to the water's edge. Firs and leafy trees were about equal in number, the stern and stately pines and firs mingling with white-trunked birches, trembling aspens, dull alders, bitter rowans, and proud maples. One rich merchant from Vishgorod had even planted chestnuts and oaks on his estate. The whole place was delightful, and all the visitors rejoiced in its beauty.

The villagers industriously ploughed their barren, stone-bestrewn fields, they prophesied the weather according to the appearance of the sky and the direction of the wind, they caught sprats in the sea, but didn't bathe themselves in it, and they let their cows wander in the forest and all along the sea-shore. In short, they behaved as the villagers in such places always do.

THE SWEET-SCENTED NAME

" Aborigines," they were called contemptuously by Professor Roggenfeldt's grandson, the schoolboy Eddy, who was an unwearied seeker after fossils.

But Madame Roggenfeldt, a grey-haired old lady, with a sweet attractive face of great former beauty, said :

" The Esthonians here are so cultured. They play Molière in their public hall, they have a choir and a band, and many of them have pianos. Their children sing and play very nicely, and on holidays they look quite like young ladies."

II

In this idyllic place one beautiful summer's day Madame Roggenfeldt was celebrating her birthday. Everything was very gay. The families of her son and daughter had all come, and the grandchildren had presented her with flowers and congratulated her prettily. Guests had come in from town, and they expected to have music and singing in the evening.

After luncheon, about three o'clock in the afternoon, there was dancing in the meadow that lay between the cliff of Très-joli and the wood on the sea-shore. The local band had been invited to play.

THE CRIMSON RIBBON

Only one old friend of the family was absent—Professor Bernard Horn—and Professor Roggenfeldt could not imagine why he had not come. He had intended to send a message to his house, but there had been no time, all the servants and everybody in the house had been very busy.

But Madame Roggenfeldt had been in a nervous and disturbed state all the morning. While the young folks were dancing she sat with her husband on a seat in the garden on the cliff and looked down at the scene below.

The sun was not too bright, the sound of the music was softened by distance, the laughter and chatter of the young people was not heard too loudly, the movements of the dancers were slow and melancholy.

Three Esthonian peasant-musicians in grey felt hats were seated one behind the other with their backs to the sea on stools placed at the edge of a square even space. Their sunburnt faces expressed the zeal of close attention and nothing else. Their sunburnt hands moved exactly and mechanically And from afar they looked like dolls placed there, parts of a very complicated musical machine.

In front of the players was a music-stand,

and behind it stood a short elderly man waving his conductor's stick calmly, confidently, and as mechanically as the players moved their hands. He too had a sunburnt neck and hands. When he moved a few steps from the stand he was seen to be very lame. And it seemed as if his lameness had been planned by an ignorant but artistic workman, fashioning this fine toy so as to be more suitable for the music of the dance.

The sounds of the music seemed extraordinarily regular and monotonous. One could have wished for some slight inaccuracy or capricious interruption of the rhythm ; but afterwards one remembered that it could not be otherwise, that such was the law of this methodically gay and yet melancholy measure.

The young men and girls sat on benches on the other two sides of the square. The fourth side had a light fence beyond which the ground sloped upward, and here upon the grass lay some onlookers who did not dance but had come to watch others dance and to listen to the music.

All the people present seemed to be under the spell of the devilishly-monotonous and inhumanly precise rhythm of this wonderfully executed music. All the young folks danced together and stepped apart with the earnestness and exactitude demanded of them by the power of the mechanical example given them by the sunburnt hand of the lame conductor beating out the time. And the spectators who looked on respectfully and the little peasant children who stood around never moved ; they looked as if they all had been carved out of the same unbending material and coloured with the same colours of amber and red-lead.

III

" Don't you think the musicians play very well, Agnes ? " asked Professor Roggenfeldt of his wife.

Agnes Rudolfovna sighed, as if she had been brought back from some sweet vision of the past :

" Yes, they play very well," said she, " especially if one remembers that they are only simple peasants."

" The peasants here have culture and so are very different from the Russian peasants," said her husband.

" Yes, indeed," said Agnes Rudolfovna.

" But I can't think why our friend, Doctor Horn, hasn't come. I feel quite anxious about him. I'm afraid he must have been taken ill suddenly. If he doesn't come soon, I think we must send and enquire about him."

Agnes Rudolfovna did not reply. She looked intently at the dancers. Her thin but still beautiful fingers trembled as she smoothed down the folds of her white dress.

It was strange and somewhat painful to look down upon this slow dance and to listen to the melancholy sounds of the waltz, played so precisely by the stiff brown hands of the musicians.

Yes, it was painful but yet sweet to the old lady to recall that far-off time when Edward and Agnes were still young, when he was a fine young man with sparkling eyes, and she a beautiful girl, beautiful as only a beloved and loving woman can be. In sweetness and in pain there revived in her soul memories of that far-off night in the happy month of May and of that old sweet wrong-doing, now long past with her departed youth.

Many years had passed away and she had kept her secret. But to-day Agnes Rudolfovna felt that the time had come when she must speak out the dreadful words of a delayed confession.

THE CRIMSON RIBBON

She had wept much during the past night, and early this morning she had risen and written a letter and sent it off to Doctor Horn.

During the morning her old friend had sent her a bouquet of flowers and an answer to her letter,—a few words written in the firm even hand of a strong-souled man, and a scrap of crimson ribbon.

And now the old lady sat by the side of her aged husband on the seat overlooking the steep cliff, looking out on to the bright greenness, on the blue of the heavens and the sea, listening to the beating of her fainting heart and preparing herself to speak. But she couldn't make up her mind to begin.

IV

A tall thin elderly gentleman in a shabby grey coat and faded grey felt hat came along, crunching the gravel of the path under his feet, and stood near the professor. He looked at the musicians and the dancers, screwing up his grey eyes to see them better. There was an expression of astonishment on his dry, nervous face.

" Pardon me," he said at last, raising his hat, " but what is this ? What band is it ? "

Professor Roggenfeldt turned his calm blue eyes on the unexpected visitor and answered with a bow of acknowledgment :

" Oh, that is the local peasant band. The villagers form their own band and they play if one invites them. Once every summer they give a concert in that field and take a collection from the audience, and with the money they buy music and pay their expenses. But the visitors here don't often hire the band and they don't get much money at their annual concert. And yet they keep up their band from year to year, and it's a wonderfully good one for a country place."

" The villagers are very musical and have some education," said Madame Roggenfeldt. " They've even got their own theatre where the young people produce classical pieces quite passably."

" Thanks very much," replied the stranger. " But don't you think they play very strangely ? "

Agnes Rudolfovna blushed slightly, smiled a little, and said quietly :

" No, I don't find it strange."

" Nor I either," said her husband.

" But," insisted the stranger, " don't you think that these people are just like wooden dolls and that they play without understanding the music just as in all probability they don't understand anything of their beautiful surroundings ? "

Agnes Rudolfovna shook her head as she answered :

" If they didn't understand the music they couldn't play so well."

" No," said the old professor, " their lack of understanding would be bound to show itself in their playing. And I think, or rather I am convinced, that they don't make any mistakes. At least my ear doesn't distinguish any false notes, and though I can't call myself a musician I understand something about music and I play a little myself."

Agnes Rudolfovna looked tenderly at her husband.

"Edward plays excellently," said she. "He has a good touch and an irreproachable ear."

Professor Roggenfeldt kissed his wife's hand and said :

" Well, well, we won't exaggerate. But they certainly play very accurately."

" Accurately ! " exclaimed the stranger. " It would be better if they made mistakes and confused the time, if only they didn't play so soullessly. Don't you think it would be better if these people didn't play at all ?

Just look at them—isn't it dreadful to watch their wooden movements ? The dancers are obliged to move stiffly and the children are as immovable as in a trance. Look, isn't it as if some cruel devil had changed human beings into marionettes ! "

Professor Roggenfeldt looked at the stranger in some perplexity, and then looking again at the musicians he said :

" I think you exaggerate a little. Of course it's not a first-class band, and Nikish is not there to conduct, but I don't think they deserve such a cruel attack."

The stranger seemed a little confused.

" No, that's true," said he. " I was exaggerating. Please forgive me. You are quite right. But it's dreadful to look upon these good devils. I must go away from such a sight."

He raised his hat again, and, walking off quickly in the direction from which he had come, was soon out of sight.

V

The old couple looked at one another and both smiled.

" What a strange person ! " said the professor."

" Yes, very strange," agreed his wife. " He expects far too much from these simple peasants. They can only do what is in their power and give what they are able to give."

" No, they can't give more," said the professor.

They were silent and looked once more at the dancers. At length Professor Roggen-feldt said :

" It's true they play without any vivacity. And the young people dance very languidly to their music. If you remember, Agnes, we used not to dance like that. The poet is right indeed when he says that the world is growing wiser, but colder."

Agnes smiled but did not reply. Her delicate youthful - looking face was again suffused with a slight blush.

Presently there came an interval between two dances. The lame conductor talked to the dancers, and a ringing voice was heard :

" A mazurka, a mazurka, please."

Agnes turned to her husband, and in a strangely agitated way began to speak.

" Edward," said she, " I used to think, or rather I used to feel, in the same way as this strange gentleman. Yes, in just the same way, and I even more than he. The

measured beat of life bored me and I did
what he advocates. I made a daring, but
a false, note."

The old professor shook his fine grey head
and smiled as he said gently :

" No, Agnes, you have played your part
well. Your partner has never been put out
of tune through your mistakes."

But the old lady showed still greater
agitation. She nearly wept as she said :

" No, no, Edward, you don't know. I
have been silent for a long time, but to-day
I have resolved to tell you all. And that's
the reason why Doctor Horn hasn't come."

And still trembling, and with difficulty
keeping back her tears, the old lady began
hurriedly to tell the story of what had happened to her so many years before, on one
clear and perfumed night of May, when she
had deceived her husband and allowed his
friend Bernard Horn to make love to her.

VI

" It was in the third year of our married
life," said Agnes. " We lived here during
the first summer, and there were few other
visitors, so it was sometimes difficult to get
provisions. But because our young friend

THE CRIMSON RIBBON

Bernard Horn—he wasn't a doctor then—often went into the town, he used to get things for us as well as for himself. You were indoors a good deal, for you were very busy then, finishing your thesis for your doctor's degree. In the evenings, when it didn't rain, we used to go for walks, and our young friend Bernard often accompanied us. One evening at the end of May you didn't want to go as usual. You were so much interested in an article in a magazine which had come that day from Brussels that we couldn't tear you away from it, and we went off by ourselves, laughing and chattering together."

"Yes, yes," said Edward Roggenfeldt quietly. "The author had so mixed his true judgments with paradoxes that even now I haven't forgotten the article. I sat over it a long time, looked up some points in several other books, and then in consequence wrote three superfluous pages of my thesis. Superfluous, that is, in comparison with my original idea, but as I think not entirely superfluous in essence."

He was silent for a few moments and then went on :

"However, half an hour after your departure I came after you. I remember it was a lovely evening. I wanted to think over some matter, and I walked along the shore where the sea made scarcely a splash on the sand. But afterwards I returned and sat down to my books again."

"Bernard and I walked to the West Cape," continued Agnes. "The sunset that night was wonderful. I don't think ever before or since have I seen such a magnificent sky, such a sea, and such clouds. Everything in front of us was flaming, all the shore was suffused with crimson as if blushing with happiness, the air was so clear, so calm, so full of rosy colour that one wanted to weep and to laugh at the same time. It was as if a pure golden light had dissolved in tears and blood, and the soul was full of rapture and sorrow. Oh, I cannot say how I felt then. I think I didn't know then what was happening to me. Some unknown force overpowered me, and I felt unable to withstand it. It was as if a curtain had been lifted from my life, as if the triumphant light of this heavenly glow had suddenly illumined in a clear light before me something which I had never noticed before—and I suddenly understood that Bernard Horn was in love with me."

Edward Roggenfeldt stroked his wife's

hand tenderly as he said in a caressing tone :

" He fell in love with you the first time he saw you."

Agnes was beginning to conquer her agitation, and her voice rang out clearly and young as she continued :

" I looked at him. I knew that I was doing wrong, but I knew that in that moment I was happy. Never for one moment, dear Edward, did I love you less. But some one powerful and insidious seemed to whisper to me that the soul of man is broad and high, that the soul of man is greater than the world, and that love knows neither bounds nor measure.

" I don't remember what we talked about, but I remember where we went. It was already beginning to get dark, for we had gone into the forest, and the midnight glow came faintly through the trees. I listened to the voice of love. I kissed Bernard Horn. I lay submissively in his arms and responded to his caresses with passionate embraces, and I laughed and wept. I laughed as I haven't known how to laugh for a long time ; I wept as I weep now."

The tears trickled gently down her cheeks.

Edward Roggenfeldt put his arms about her and soothed her, saying :

"Don't weep. Don't weep, my dear Agnes. You have been a faithful wife to me."

And she, weeping bitterly, restraining her tears no longer, continued :

"I was false to you, my dear one, on that passionate, that beautiful night. I lost my senses, and what I did then seemed neither dreadful nor shameful. I leant on Bernard's arm as we walked home from the forest, and I listened to him and talked to him and was not ashamed nor fearful. When we parted near our house I gave him the crimson ribbon I wore for a memory. And he has kept it all these years."

VII

Agnes was silent for a moment. Her eyes held a rapturous expression, and dilated as she gazed before her. Her face showed the remembrance of past happiness. Presently she went on :

"The next day I came to myself. I was overcome by shame and terror. I was utterly unlike myself all day. Bernard came as usual in the evening. He was thoughtful and confused. He looked me straight in the eyes and understood what I was feeling, and it grieved him. I seized a moment when we were alone together to say, ' Dear Bernard, we have done very wrong. I forgot my duty ; I broke faith with my husband whom I love truly and devotedly. I don't know what happened to me,' I said to him, ' but when we were together yesterday I felt as if I loved you.' "

" You have always loved him, Agnes, since the first time you saw him," said her husband in a very quiet gentle tone.

Agnes trembled a little. She wanted to look up at her husband, but could not, and she went on hurriedly :

" ' I am very sinful,' I said to Bernard Horn, ' because I love you both, my dear husband and you. This is a great sin in the sight of God and of men,' I said, ' a sin, because a wife ought to be faithful to her husband, and he to her. Dear Bernard,' said I to him, ' I shall always cherish the sweet memory of last night, but what happened then must never be repeated, and I must never again walk alone with you on this beautiful shore. And you, dear Bernard, must give me your word that you will never ask me what I cannot give you, and you won't expect kisses from me.' I wept as I spoke to him, like a little girl, and my heart was torn with grief and with a strange joy. I knew my sin, and my contrite heart trembled in my bosom. I repented, and in that moment I knew that He who had given me a heart to love and to be happy had forgiven me. Bernard looked lovingly at me, and I saw that he was touched to the depths of his soul. He kissed my hand and said, ' Don't take away the crimson ribbon from me, dear Agnes,' and I whispered back, ' Keep it,' and ran away to my own room. For a long time I wept there, and I wanted to weep endlessly. But I remembered that I must see after the supper, and I came downstairs, after carefully bathing my swollen eyelids in cold water."

Agnes was silent, and with a timid imploring gaze looked up at her husband. The eyes of the old man glowed as radiantly as in his youth. He put his arm around his wife tenderly and said :

" I remember that day, dear Agnes. I remember it, because I knew all. I saw you and I understood everything."

" You knew ! " exclaimed Agnes quietly. " You knew, and said nothing to me ! "

THE CRIMSON RIBBON

" I knew," said Professor Roggenfeldt, " that you said nothing to me about the matter for fear of hurting me. I trusted you ; I knew you were loyal to me ; and if you did sin against me then I forgave you before you realised that it was a sin. Like this old gentleman who was here just now, I was ready to forgive deviation from rhythm, and even a mistake in the playing, if only the playing were not without soul. But you have always warmed and enlightened my life. You have not been like these mechanical musicians who have learned by heart their parts, which never express their souls. I have been happy with you, because you have given me the rapture of love."

" My dear one, my beloved," said she, touched by his words, " I knew that you had a great and a beautiful soul. It's true, I didn't want to grieve you. But now that so many years have passed, and we have not much longer to live in this beautiful world, I resolved at last to tell you all. This morning I wrote to Doctor Horn, and at my request he sent me back the crimson ribbon. I put it on your writing-table after lunch, before we came out here. It is yours."

" No, no," answered Edward with animation. " Our dear friend, Doctor Bernard Horn, must keep it. He has done us much service, and he was with you in that fateful moment when your heart was surcharged with an unreasonable, immeasurable love. He held a cup of sweet wine to your thirsty lips, and may God bless him for this as I bless him for it. But now, Agnes, dry your tears and send at once to Bernard. He must come to-day and bring his violin, and we again . . ."

VIII

By this time the music below had come to an end. The young folks, laughing and talking noisily together, were climbing upwards along the sloping road that wound along the steep cliff.

Edward and Agnes walked slowly homeward. There was a sweet delicate fragrance of eglantine in the air, pale peonies fluttered their rosy double petals, the first poppies crimsoned and flamed on the long beds under the windows. Over the straggling dark green of the wild vine on the terrace was borne the fragrance of stocks. Wonderful tuberoses dreamed unceasingly, exhaling an infinite fragrance of happiness immeasurable and of love without end.

On the threshold of their home Edward Roggenfeldt paused for a moment and said :

" Yes, he is right. These wooden musicians are terrible. I'm glad we can't hear them playing any longer. But you and I, Agnes, have not played our part in life without inspiration ! "

Slayers of Innocent Babes

HAVING with great success quelled the rebellion of those who had refused to offer sacrifice and bow before the effigy of the god - like emperor, the detachment of Roman horse returned to camp. Much blood had been shed, many of those disrespectful unto Caesar had been slain, and the tired soldiers looked forward impatiently to the joyful hour when they could get to their tents, where they could without disturbance take delight in the company of the wives and daughters that they had borne off from the villages of the rebellious.

These women and maids, seized at the very moment of the slaying of their husbands and fathers, at the moment of the burning of their farms, lay bound on straw at the bottom of the heavy carts drawn by stout horses, and they had been sent on in advance by the direct road to the camp.

The horsemen themselves had chosen a

roundabout road home, for, according to the Centurion, several of the insurgent villagers had taken to flight and hidden themselves in out-of-the-way parts, and he thought to come up with some of them and despatch them. For though their swords had been made into long-toothed saws by the fighting and were covered with blood, though their spears were blunted with hard work, their Roman appetite still craved the fresh hot blood of further victims.

It was a sultry day, and the hottest hour of the day, just afternoon. The sky was cloudlessly and mercilessly bright. The fiery Dragon of the sky quivering with fury poured streams of fierce rage into the vast and tired emptiness. The withered grass held to the thirsting and parched earth, and grieved with her, and lay stifling under the hot dust.

Smoke of dust rose from the horses' feet and remained a cloud in the still air. The dust settled on the armour of the tired horsemen and gave a dull glimmer of velvet to their accoutrements. Through the clouds of their own dust the country through which they passed seemed portentous, gloomy, melancholy.

Earth herself, burned up by the fierce

Dragon, lay submissive under the horses' hoofs. The empty road trembled and jingled under the blows of the iron horseshoes.

At rare intervals they came upon poor villages and collections of wretched huts, but the Centurion, overcome by the heat, relented in his purpose of searching out those who might be in hiding. As he sat in his saddle, jogging rhythmically with his horse's movement, he thought merely of the end of the journey, the escape from the heat, the cool tent, the night tide, the new bride.

A young soldier, however, interrupted his thoughts, saying :

" Over there by the roadside I see a crowd of people. Order us, Marcellus, and we will whirl down upon them and scatter them. The wind which our horses will make will disperse the stupor into which the heat has cast us, and will fan away the dust and tiredness from both you and us."

The Centurion cast his sharp gaze in the direction indicated by the soldier, and looked attentively.

" No, Lucillus," said he, smiling, " that crowd is a crowd of children playing by the roadside. It's not worth chasing them. Let them look at our fine horses, at our gallant troop, and so gain in early years a strong impression of the grandeur of the Roman arms and the fame of our unconquerable and godlike Caesar."

Young Lucillus did not dare to object to the Centurion's words. But his face grew dark. He dropped back into his accustomed position in the troop and said in a whisper to his neighbour, also a young man :

" These children are perhaps the offspring of that same rebellious gang. I'd cut them up with joy. Our Centurion has become too sensitive and is losing the true valour of a soldier."

But his friend replied in displeasure : " Why should we fight with children ? What glory would there be in that ? It is enough for us to fight with those who can defend themselves."

Lucillus thereupon turned red and was silent.

The soldiers approached the children. The children ceased their game and stood at the side of the road and gazed at the soldiers, wondering at their fine horses, at their shining armour, their sunburnt faces. They wondered, lisped, stared—stared with widely-opened eyes.

Suddenly one of the children, the beautiful

boy Lin, cried out an unexpected word, and his black eyes glowed with sacred rage :

" Murderers ! "

And he pointed his little hand at the Centurion, who for his part went past gloomily, not hearing what the child said.

The children, frightened at the words of little Lin, crowded round him and implored him not to say anything more. And they whispered :

" Let's run, else they'll kill us all."

And the girls began to cry. But beautiful Lin got free of the little crowd and fearlessly shook his fist in the faces of the soldiers, and once more cried out :

" Executioners ! Torturers of innocent people ! "

His black eyes glowed with rage and he repeated his cries :

" Executioners ! Executioners ! "

The children wailed aloud in order to smother the sound of the boy's words, and several of them took him by the arms and drew him away, but he broke away from them and turned to the horsemen of the emperor and cursed them once more.

The horsemen stopped, and the youngest of them exclaimed :

" Spawn of unbelievers. They've got the taint in their hearts. They ought to be destroyed. There's no room in the world for those who insult the Roman warrior."

And even the older soldiers went to the Centurion and said :

" The impudence of these rascals deserves condign punishment. Command us to go after them and slaughter them. We should destroy the unbelievers whilst they are young and weak, for when they grow up they will be capable of combining and doing much damage."

And the Centurion yielded and said :

" You go after them, kill those who shouted at us and punish the rest, so that they may remember to the end of their days what it means to insult the Roman soldier."

And the Centurion and the troop of horse turned back and galloped through the dust after the children.

Lin saw the soldiers coming after them and cried to the others :

" Leave me. You cannot save me, but if we all flee together then we shall all be killed by this dishonourable and pitiless troop. I will go and meet them. They will kill me only, and I have no wish to go on living in a world where such ugly things are done."

Lin stopped, and his tired and frightened companions could not drag him further. They all came to a standstill and the horsemen quickly came up and surrounded them.

The drawn swords gleamed in the sunlight. The children trembled, burst into sobs, and clung close together in a bunch.

The fiery Dragon of the sky urged the soldiers to murder, inflamed their blood, and was ready even to kiss the innocent blood of the children and to breathe his sultry heat upon their dismembered bodies. But the boy Lin came bravely forth from the crowd and thus addressed the Centurion :

" Old man, it was I who called your men murderers and executioners, I who cursed you and called down vengeance from the true lord upon you. These others are only children trembling and weeping. They are afraid that your wicked men will kill them and that they will follow and kill our fathers and mothers. They are submissive unto you. Therefore, if you are not yet sated with murder, kill me only. I am not afraid of you; I hate you. I despise your sword and your unjust sway over our country. I do not wish to live on the earth which is

194

trampled by the horses of your false troops. My hands are weak, and I am not yet tall enough to fight you or I would. So kill me whilst you have the chance."

The Centurion listened in astonishment, but answered :

" No, cockatrice, not as you will but as I will. You shall die, but not you only."

And to the troops he said :

" Kill them all. Don't leave one of the serpent brood alive. The words of this bold boy will have fallen as seed in their hearts. Kill them all without mercy, big and little, babes also."

The soldiers fell upon them and cut them to bits with their merciless swords. The gloomy valley and the dusty road became tremblingly vocal with children's shrieks. The misty horizon echoed painfully, and echoed again and was silent. The horses deflated their nostrils and smelt the smoking blood, and with their iron-shod hoofs they trod on the poor bodies.

Then the warriors returned to the road laughing joyfully and cruelly. They hastened homeward to their camp conversing and rejoicing.

But the road went on, still went on dusty as ever, ravaged by the fiery eyes of the

Dragon. Afternoon turned to evening and the Dragon effaced himself in shadow, but there came no evening coolness. The wind, as if enchanted by silence and fear, lay asleep. The sultry Dragon sinking into darkness looked in the eyes of the Centurion and seemed to smile a calm and dreadful smile. The twilight was calm and sultry and shadowy; the beat of the horses' feet was even and rhythmical and drowsy, and the Centurion felt sad at heart.

So measured was the beat of the sounding hoofs, and so grey, so hopeless and unlifting was the column of dust in which they moved, that it seemed as if they were on an endless journey. The greyer became the night the more lonely and remote they seemed, and the empty clangour of their beating hoofs resounded in the far distance of the wilderness. A sense of dread came over him, a dread to which as to his tiredness he saw no term.

He seemed to hear the sounds of wailing somewhere afar.

The earth trembled and murmured under the beat of the horses' hoofs.

Some one was running towards them.

A dim voice, a voice like that of the boy began to cry.

SLAYERS OF INNOCENT BABES

The Centurion looked round on his soldiers. The shadow of night lay on their bowed faces, distorted with dust, sunken with tiredness, and a look of confused terror hung on their countenances.

The parched lips of Lucillus whispered nervously, " Oh that the camp were in sight."

" What is it, Lucillus ? " asked the Centurion looking fixedly into the tired face of the young soldier.

And Lucillus whispered in reply :

" I am in dread."

And then, blushing to have confessed to fear, he added in a louder voice :

" It's terribly hot."

And then relapsing into a whisper, he shuddered and went on.

" That accursed boy is on my conscience, his face pursues me. He was in league with sorcerers, and though we cut him down we could not lay him, he was enchanted . . ."

The Centurion scanned the dark landscape. There was not a soul to be seen, near or far.

" Have you lost the amulet you received from the old priest at Carthage ? I remember it was said that he who wore that amulet was immune from the spells of night enchantments," said the Centurion.

"I am wearing it now," said the young man. "But it is burning into my chest. There are earth-fiends after us; I hear the murmur of the earth disgorging the hurrying fiends."

"Oh, you make a mistake," said the Centurion, seeking to reassure him by reasonable words. "The earth fiends are mightily beholden unto us for giving them a rich feast to-day. In any case, fear should find no place in the heart of a valiant soldier, not even the fear engendered by the moaning of sprites in the night in the wilderness."

"Oh, I fear, I fear," cried Lucillus. "I hear the voice of that strange child following us."

Then suddenly in the sultry silence of the night a moaning and maledictory voice broke forth :

"Curses . . . curses upon the heads of the murderers."

The soldiers shuddered, spurred their horses and clattered along more quickly. But the voice of an unseen spirit pursued them and cried out all about them, now in front of them, now behind, now at one side, now another, sharply, distinctly :

"Murderers ! Slayers of innocent babes !

198

Merciless soldiers ; ye yourselves shall not
receive mercy ! "

The soldiers took fright and spurred their
steeds and hastened. But the old Centurion
was angry and scolded them, crying :

" For shame ! Of whom are you afraid.
Are soldiers of the mighty and godlike
Emperor afraid of shadows. From whom
do you flee ? From a boy whom you killed,
from a dead body raised to life by unclean
charms ! Pull yourselves together, men, and
remember that the Roman arms triumph not
only over our enemies, but over the enchantments of the enemy also."

The soldiers took shame. At the bidding
of the Centurion they came to a halt. They
were still and listened to the noises of the
night. Some one was distinctly on their
tracks following after them, waiting and
denouncing. No shape was seen in the
darkness or upon the vague shadowiness of
the landscape, but a small intense voice of
a child cried out incessantly.

" Let us find out who it is," said one
soldier, and the troop spurred their horses
across the waste in the direction of the
sound. And when they had lost sight of
the road they came suddenly upon a strange
child running on the heath, his garments

torn, his dark hair dabbled in blood. And the child streaming blood as he ran, moaned and shouted and threatened with a maledictory hand.

With wild rage the soldiers drew their swords and dashed at the boy and slew him again, hacking him into a hundred bits and trampling the flesh under their horses' feet. And before they resumed their journey they scattered the remains of the dead child's body and flung portions north, south, east, and west.

Then they wiped their swords in the grass, got into their saddles, and hastened once more onward on the long roundabout homeward road. But hardly had they resumed their journey than the moody silence that was between them and around them was broken by a sharp exclamation : "Murderers!" and once more they were assailed by a running accompaniment of curses and denunciation from an unseen child.

They turned their horses in terror and rage, and sought the spirit out again, and away in the darkness once more they saw the strange boy running with torn garments and black hair dabbled in blood, with blood streaming from his hands. And once more they set upon him and cut him down, and stamped upon the body and scattered the severed limbs and galloped away.

But again and again the wailing child came after them. And in the rage of murder that had no end and of wails and denunciations that never ceased the troop missed the way to the Camp and went round and round the wild district where the children had been slain by them. The grandeur of night spread over the valley and the stars glimmered, sinless, innocent, remote.

The soldiers followed on their own tracks, and the cries of the boy on the heath were heavy on their souls. Round and round they wandered and killed in fury and yet could not kill.

At last, just before sunrise, with madness at their heels the troop galloped on to the shore of the sea. And the waves boiled under the frenzied onrush of the horses.

So perished all the horsemen and with them the Centurion Marcellus.

And to the far silent spot where by the roadway lay the bodies of the boy Lin and the other children, blood-stained, unburied, wolves came creeping stealthily, fearfully, and they sated themselves with the innocent and sweet bodies of the children.

The Herald of the Beast

I

I T was quiet and peaceful, neither gladness nor sadness was in the room. The electric light was on. The walls seemed solid, firm as adamant, indestructible. The window was hidden behind heavy dark green curtains, and the big door opposite the window was locked and bolted, as was also the little one in the wall at the side. But on the other side of the doors all was dark and empty, in the wide corridor and in the melancholy hall where beautiful palms yearned for their southern homes.

Gurof was lying on the green divan. In his hands was a book. He read it, but often stopped short in his reading. He thought, mused, dreamed—and always about the same thing, always about *them*.

They were near him. He had long since noticed that. They had hid themselves. *They* were inescapably near. They

202

rustled round about, almost inaudibly, but for a long time did not show themselves to his eyes. Gurof saw the first one a few days ago; he wakened tired, miserable, pallid, and as he lazily turned on the electric light so as to expel the wild gloom of the winter morning he suddenly saw one of them.

A wee grey one, agile and furtive pattered over his pillow, lisped something, and hid himself.

And afterwards, morning and evening, they ran about Gurof, grey, agile, furtive.

And to-day he had expected them.

Now and then his head ached slightly. Now and then he was seized by cold fits and by waves of heat. Then from a corner ran out Fever long and slender, with ugly yellow face and dry bony hands, lay down beside him, embraced him, kissed his face and smiled. And the rapid kisses of the caressing and subtle Fever and the soft aching movements in his head were pleasant to him.

Weakness poured itself into all his limbs. And tiredness spread over them. But it was pleasant. The people he knew in the world became remote, uninteresting, entirely superfluous. He felt he would like to remain here with *them*.

THE SWEET-SCENTED NAME

Gurof had been indoors for several days. He had locked himself up in the house. He permitted no one to see him. Sat by himself. Thought of them. Waited them.

II

Strangely and unexpectedly the languor of sweet waiting was broken. There was a loud knocking at an outer door and then the sound of even unhurrying footsteps in the hall.

As Gurof turned his face to the door a blast of cold air swept in, and he saw, as he shivered, a boy of a wild and strange appearance. He was in a linen cloak, but showed half his body naked, and his arms were bare. His body was brown, all sunburnt. His curly hair was black and bright; black also were his eyes and sparkling. A wonderfully correct and beautiful face. But of a beauty terrible to look upon. Not a kind face, not an evil one.

Gurof was not astonished at the boy's coming. Some dominant idea had possession of his mind. And he heard how *they* crept out of sight and hid themselves.

And the boy said :

" Aristomakh ! Have you forgotten your

promise ? Do noble people act thus ? You fled from me when I was in mortal danger. You promised me something, which it seems you did not wish to fulfil. Such a long time I've been looking for you ! And behold I find you living in festivity, drowning in luxury."

Gurof looked distrustfully at the half-naked beautiful boy and a confused remembrance awakened in his soul. Something long since gratefully buried in oblivion rose up with indistinct feature and asking for remembrance tired his memory. The enigma could not be guessed though it seemed near and familiar.

And where were the unwavering walls ? Something was happening round about him, some change was taking place, but Gurof was so obsessed by the struggle with his ancient memory that he failed to take stock of those changes. He said to the wonderful boy :

" Dear boy, tell me clearly and simply without unnecessary reproaches what it was I promised you and when it was I left you in mortal danger. I swear to you by all that is holy my honour would never have allowed me to commit the ignoble act with which for some reason you charge me."

THE SWEET-SCENTED NAME

The boy nodded, and then in a loud melodious voice gave answer :

" Aristomakh ! You always were clever at verbal exercises, and indeed as clever in actions demanding daring and caution. If I said that you left me in a moment of mortal danger it is not a reproach. And I don't understand why you speak of your honour. The thing purposed by us was difficult and dangerous, but why do you quibble about it. Who is here that you think you can deceive by pretending ignorance of what happened this morning before sunrise and of the promise you had given me ? "

The electric light became dim. The ceiling seemed dark and high. There was the scent of a herb in the room—but what herb ? Its forgotten name had one time sounded sweetly on his ear. On the wings of the scent a cool air seemed wafted into the room. Gurof stood up and cried out :

" What thing did we purpose ? I deny nothing, dear boy, but I simply don't know of what you are speaking. I don't remember."

It seemed to Gurof that the child was at one and the same time both looking at him and not looking at him. Though the boy's eyes were directed towards him they seemed to be staring at some other unearthly person whose body coincided with his but who was not he.

It grew dark around him and the air became fresher and cooler. A gladness leapt in his soul and a lightness as of elementary existence. The room disappeared from his remembrance. Above he saw the stars glittering in the black sky. Once more the boy addressed him :

" We ought to have killed the Beast. I shall remind you of that when under the myriad eyes of the all-seeing sky you are again confused with fear. And how not have fear ! The thing that we purposed was great and dreadful, and it would have given a glory to our names in far posterity."

In the night quietude he heard the murmuring and gentle tinkling of a brook. He could not see the brook, but he felt that it was deliciously and tantalisingly near. They were standing in the shadow of spreading trees, and the conversation went on. Gurof asked :

" Why do you say that I left you in a moment of mortal danger ? Am I the sort of man to take fright and run away ? "

The boy laughed, and like music was his laughter. Then in sweet melodious accents he replied :

THE SWEET-SCENTED NAME

" Aristomakh, how cleverly you pretend to have forgotten all ! But I don't understand why you take the trouble to exercise such cunning, or why you contrive reproaches against yourself which I for my part should not have thought of alone. You left me in the moment of mortal danger because it was clearly necessary, and you couldn't help me otherwise than by abandoning me there. Surely you won't remain obstinate in your denial after I remind you of the words of the oracle."

Gurof suddenly remembered. It was as if a bright light had flooded into the dark abyss of the forgotten. And he cried out loudly and excitedly :

" He alone will kill the Beast ! "

The boy laughed. Aristomakh turned to him with the question :

" Have you killed the Beast, Timaride ? "

" With what ? Even were my hands strong enough I am not he who has the power to kill the Beast with a blow of the fist. We were incautious, Aristomakh, and without weapons. We were playing on the sands and the Beast fell upon us suddenly and struck me with his heavy paw. My fate was to give my life as a sweet sacrifice to glory and in high exploit, but to you it remained to finish the work. And whilst the Beast tore my helpless body you might have run, swift-footed Aristomakh, might have gained your spear, and you might have struck the Beast whilst he was drunk with my blood. But the Beast did not accept my sacrifice ; I lay before him motionless and looked up at his blood-weltering eyes, and he kept me pinned to the ground by the heavy paw on my shoulder. He breathed hotly and unevenly and he growled softly, but he did not kill me. He simply licked over my face with his broad warm tongue and went away."

" Where is he now ? " asked Aristomakh.

The night air felt moist and calm, and through it came the musical answer of Timaride :

" I rose when he had left me but he was attracted by the scent of my blood and followed after me. I don't know why he has set upon me again. Still I am glad that he follows, for so I bring him to you. Get the weapon that you so cleverly hid, and kill the Beast, and I in my turn will run away and leave you in the moment of mortal danger, face to face with the enraged Beast. Good luck, Aristomakh ! "

And saying that Timaride ran away, his

white cloak gleaming but a minute in the darkness. And just as he disappeared there broke out the horrible roaring of the Beast and the thud of his heavy paws on the ground. Thrusting to right and left the foliage of the bushes there appeared in the darkness the immense monstrous head of the Beast, and his large eyes gleamed like luminous velvet. The Beast ceased to roar, and with his eyes fixed on Aristomakh approached him stealthily and silently.

Terror filled the heart of Aristomakh.

" Where is the spear ? " he whispered, and immediately he turned to flee. But with a heavy bound the Beast started after him, roaring and bellowing, and pulled him down. And when the Beast held him a great yell broke through the stillness of the night. Then Aristomakh moaned out the ancient and horrible words of the curse of the walls.

And up rose the walls about him. . . .

III

The walls of the room stood firm, un-wavering, and the barely reflected electric light seemed to die upon them. All the rest of the room was customary and usual.

THE HERALD OF THE BEAST

Once more Fever came and kissed him with dry yellow lips and caressed him with wizened bony hands. The same tedious little book with little white pages lay on the table, and in the green divan lay Gurof, and Fever embraced him, scattering rapid kisses with hurrying lips. And once more the grey ones rustled and chattered.

Gurof raised his head a little as if with great effort and said hollowly :

" The curse of the walls."

What was he talking about ? What curse ? What was the curse ? What were the words of it ? Were there any ?

The little ones, grey and agile, danced about the book and turned with their tails the pallid pages, and with little squeaks and whimpers answered him :

" Our walls are strong. We live in the walls. No fear troubles us inside the walls."

Among them was a singular looking one, not at all like the rest. He was quite black and wore dress of mingled smoke and flame. From his eyes came little lightnings. Suddenly he detached himself from the others and stood before Gurof who cried out :

" Who are you ? What do you want ? "

The black guest replied :

" I . . . am the Herald of the Beast.

THE SWEET-SCENTED NAME

On the shore of the forest stream you left long since the mangled body of Timaride. The Beast has sated himself with the fine blood of your friend—he has devoured the flesh which should have tasted earthly happiness ; the wonderful human form has been destroyed, and that in it which was more than human has perished, all to give a moment's satisfaction to the ever insatiable Beast. The blood, the marvellous blood, godly wine of joy, the wine of more than human blessing—where is it now ? Alas ! the eternally thirsting Beast has been made drunk for a moment by it. You have left the mangled body of Timaride by the side of the forest stream, have forgotten the promise given to your splendid friend, and the word of the ancient oracle has not driven fear from your heart. Think you then, that saving yourself you can escape the Beast and that he will not find you ? ''

The voice and the words were stern. The grey ones had stopped in their dancing to listen. Gurof said :

'' What is the Beast to me. I have fixed my walls about me for ever, and the Beast will not find a way to me in my fortress.''

At that the grey ones rejoiced and scampered round the room anew, but the Herald of the Beast cried out once more, and sharp and stern were his accents :

" Do you not see that I am here. I am here because I have found you. I am here because the curse of the walls has lost power. I am here because Timaride is waiting and tirelessly questioning. Do you not hear the gentle laughter of the brave and trusting child ? Do you not hear the roaring of the Beast ? "

From beyond the wall broke out the terrible roaring of the Beast.

" But the walls are firm for ever by the spell I cast, my fortress cannot be destroyed," cried Gurof.

And the Black One answered, imperiously :

" I tell thee, man, the curse of the walls is dead. But if you don't believe, but still think you can save yourself, pronounce the curse again."

Gurof shuddered. He indeed believed that the curse was dead, and all that was around him whispered to him the terrible news. The Herald of the Beast had pronounced the fearful truth. Gurof's head ached, and he felt weary of the hot kisses that clinging, caressing Fever still gave him. The words of the sentence seemed to strain his consciousness, and the Herald of the

Beast as he stood before him was magnified
until he obscured the light and stood like a
great shadow over him, and his eyes glowed
like fires.

Suddenly the black cloak fell from the
shoulders of the visitor and Gurof recognised
him—it was the child Timaride.

"Are you going to kill the Beast?"
asked Timaride in a high-sounding voice.
"I have brought him to you. The malicious
gift of godhead will avail you no longer, for
the curse is dead. It availed you once,
making as nothing my sacrifice and hiding
from your eyes the glory of your exploit.
But to-day the tune is changed, dead is the
curse, get your sword quickly and kill the
Beast. I was only a child; now I have
become the Herald of the Beast. I have fed
the Beast with my blood but he thirsts
anew. To you I have brought him, and do
you fulfil your promise and kill him. Or
die."

He vanished.

The walls shuddered at the dreadful
roaring. The room filled with airs that were
cold and damp.

The wall directly opposite the place where
Gurof lay collapsed, and there entered the
ferocious, immense, and monstrous Beast.

THE HERALD OF THE BEAST

With fearful bellowing he crept up to Gurof and struck him on the chest with his paw. The merciless claws went right into his heart. An awful pain shattered his body. And looking at him with gleaming bloody eyes the Beast crouched over Gurof, grinding his bones in his teeth and devouring his yet-beating heart.

On the Other Side of the River Mairure

I

THE two weeks spent by my brother Sin and myself in the magnificent capital, a vicious if splendid city, passed by as quickly and confusedly as the story of a dream. It was astonishing and bewildering to us, this proud imperial city full of human ingenuity and enticement, and we felt far from it, not only because our native villages were far away, but because our morals and customs were further still removed. Alack, too late I learned that the town was not simply wonderful, glorious, noisy, populous, but also fearsone and terrible to the young untried heart fresh with the innocence of the country. It was my fate to endure incomparable temptation and mortification. But my young brother ! Ah, that I had never brought him with me to this place !

THE RIVER MAIRURE

Our friend Sarroo, with whom we stayed, wished to show us some return for the hospitality which he enjoyed when he had been staying some time back up in our own country. He gave himself up to us entirely, and we were, you may say, inseparable ; he put himself to infinite trouble that we might miss nothing in this great and wonderful town. Other men await the departure of their guests with scarcely feigned impatience, but our good friend was even mortified because we could not stay the whole year round with him and witness the cycle of pageants, festivities, and offerings of sacrifice.

Sarroo showed us everything : the temples of gracious and ingracious gods, the woods sacred to mysterious spirits, the dark towers of tranquillity, the sweet-smelling gardens of voluptuous delight, the taverns where caresses may be bought for money, bazaars full of beautiful cloth and carpets, weapons, precious stones, perfumes, chattering birds, monkeys, slaves of all skins and colours, from delicate rose to darkest black, coffee-houses, shows — strange sights without number. But the calamity that befell us lay not in the many things that we saw. I have not yet mentioned the singular temptation that involved ourselves and our villages in the greatest unhappiness.

O that I had never visited that town ! Or that I had not brought with me a child so weak to withstand temptation !

One morning our friend Sarroo said to us : " To-day I will show you the imperial menagerie "—at that time the menagerie might be seen not only by ourselves but by foreigners.

My brother Sin agreed with shouts of pleasure. I, for my part, hesitated, for I had had, the night before, a dream in which I saw a beast of immeasurable power and fierceness, whose roaring was like that of him who dwells in the woods on the other side of the river Mairure. And I did not wish to visit the accursed beast-garden, but I did not like to offend our kind host.

II

First of all we wandered through a park which seemed almost limitless in extent, and we saw a marvellous diversity of birds all shut in cages. We saw gigantic birds with great wings able to carry in their talons fat sheep, and we saw birds almost devoid of wings, but of wonderfully beautiful plumage which reminded us of the luminous stones which we find in the sand of the river Mairure, birds whose melodious singing charmed our ears, even birds who could speak the language of that land, but not very well, though quite loudly and distinctly.

In immense tanks we saw the wonders of the seas and the rivers. In cages and glass-houses we saw poisonous adders and immense cobras—they distended their jaws with such rage, and thrusting out their dreadful stings we trembled involuntarily. Before their eyes we quailed, and at moments seemed rooted to the ground before their gaze. They say that their teeth and poison-bags have been removed, otherwise visitors might yet be drawn to their death by the power of the serpents' eyes.

And we saw innumerable beasts both fierce and gentle, camels with two humps, rhinoceroses, hippopotamuses, unheard - of beasts with terrible claws, monsters with noses like serpents.

My young brother Sin was elated by the sights. I for my part, under the influence of such a variety of impressions and emotions, revolting odours and appalling sounds, grew more and more confused.

" In a minute I will show you a beast that

is truly royal," said our friend Sarroo at length; but before he had time to tell us its name I was overcome by an inexplicable emotion, and I heard a sound which forced me to fling myself on my face on the ground. Out of all the mingled cries and voices of the menagerie there suddenly rose up a threatening roar—the voice of the dweller in the woods on the other side of the Mairure.

That roar, in the quiet of our village nights, had often broken on our hearts telling us that the dwellers of the woods thirsted anew for a victim, and behold we heard it in the menagerie of the Great Emperor. Lying prostrate on the ground I waited that he should make his choice, and my heart was full of terror. I said good-bye to life— never had I heard that roaring so near to me before.

Then whilst my brother and I lay there in the dust and waited, we heard a noise louder than the roaring of the beast—the laughter of the people in the garden, and our friend Sarroo, laughing like the rest, tried to raise us from the earth.

" Don't fear," said he, " the beast is only dangerous when it is free. It is now imprisoned in a cage, and couldn't get out of it

even were it five times as strong as it is.
The man who made the cage knew his work.
And think, friends, how could there be any
danger from the beasts in the king's pleasure-
ground ? "

Then, not raising my head, I answered
my friend Sarroo : " My heart knows not
fear, and does not tremble even in moments
of mortal danger, but I heard the roar of
the dweller in the woods on the other side
of the river Mairure, and at that sound it
becomes a man to lie in the dust and
wait till the choice of a victim has been
made."

Then, laughing as before, Sarroo replied :
" That is only a beast in a cage roaring, and
it is quite harmless. Look ! Even little
children go right up to the cage and are
not afraid ; the wire cannot be broken.
The beast is fed by the keepers, and the
meat they give him he has, and no more."

As I lay in the dust the roaring continued.
I remembered the many nights in the village
when, awakening in my tent, I heard the
same awful demands for a victim, and I
dared not get up. But at last I heard my
brother Sin say to me, " I have dared to
look up ; it seems the roaring proceeds
from a beast shut in a cage."

Hearing that, I did not know what to think or what to do. Had any demon such power as to dare to imitate his threatening roar ? Could demons dare so much, were they so strong ? Did the dweller on the other side of the river Mairure conceal himself in the hide of an imprisoned and harmless beast ? did he mock the pitiful blind people who looked at him and from them make choice of a victim ? But could the great and stern one descend to such a degree as to hide himself in the skin of a caught beast ? Or could it be thought that the contemptible demon of this dishonourable town had wrought a spell ?

Did it not augur innumerable misfortunes for myself and my brother Sin that we dared to take part in the false triumph of the people of this debauched and cursed city, even though we lay humbly in the dust before the horrible cage ? And what meant this fearful, overwhelming thing ? It was incomprehensible to us, perhaps altogether beyond the understanding of the weak mind of man. At least it was insulting to the covenants of our blessed country.

Then whilst I lay in the dust, and the dishonourable made mock of us, my brother Sin said to me :

THE RIVER MAIRURE

" Let us go hence."

But was it possible to go whilst he roared over us ? And what if I saw him whom none of us had ever looked in the face ? If it were indeed he, how could we go away and how could we leave him there in shame and insult ? But staying, did we not share in the most disgusting of human sins ? I resolved to go ; there was no way else, though such a thought had been so far from me when first the roaring broke upon our ears.

But first, before I rose, I carefully covered up the face of my brother Sin with my cloak, for I thought if one of us must perish meeting the enraged gaze let it be the elder of us, for he, my brother, had yet to taste the sweetest moments of life. And I also thought he might perhaps do something rash, and having seen once, by accident and without retribution might on his own account dare to look a second time, and I know by experience that it is madness to tempt Fate.

So we slunk out of the gardens followed by the coarse and laughing crowd. Truly that people, their accursed city, and its walls crowned by towers, are worthy of a great punishment !

THE SWEET-SCENTED NAME

III

That very day we laded our camels, and before sunset had left the horrible town.

We had much time on the way to think on what had happened to us at the menagerie of the Great Emperor. But the phenomenon entirely baffled us.

It was not necessary to think that it portented evil and frightful misfortune, nor could we take it as a sign of blessing. Do we ever hear of the most powerful one appearing with the single object of being a sign to man ? No, when even in the most ancient traditions, true, it has been handed down that the dweller on the other side of the river Mairure showed himself as a sign of impending calamity or blessing, or that he came to prophesy at all—he always came roaring threateningly, and took the one of us on whom his choice fell.

For a long time we wandered through the desert saying not a word to one another. I knew by my brother's gloomy silence that he also thought on what had happened. At last, when we were but three days' journey from home, he broke silence, saying, " Whilst we lay on the ground and the people laughed at us, and I lifted my head, I saw the open jaws of the beast. There could be no mistake, the roaring proceeded from one of the caught beasts that were shut in the cages."

And I said to my brother Sin :

" Of such bodeful appearances it is better to be silent. So our forefathers enjoined. There is much in the world that is inexplicable, and even if it is possible to consider it familiarly and without fear, we ought always to hold ourselves humbly and reverently toward it."

Sin was a long time without words, but towards sunset he broke silence, saying : " It was the same roaring which we heard outside our village when he came for a victim. He to whom we prostrate ourselves with such humility and who has devoured countless delicate girls and pretty children is a wild beast with green cat's eyes, with yellow hide sown all over with black spots. And it is possible to catch him and put him in a cage."

I was horrified, and forbade my brother Sin to speak such dishonouring words. But Sin was possessed of the spirit that eternally strives against the dweller on the other side of the river Mairure, and he turned upon me in rage and cried out :

" I saw that it was a wild beast. Why should we make any more sacrifices to him ? Can we not also build a cage for him—a worthy chamber—and make him live peacefully there, so saving ourselves and our families from terror and death ? I am not so mad as to think that we can live without him, but why not feed him on the flesh of sheep or bulls ? Why should we weep for our children when he can make such an excellent repast on cattle ? "

In vain I forbade my brother, in vain did I mercilessly beat him, his tongue continued to utter the same lying and dishonourable words.

And we returned home.

IV

Soon the young people of our village began to hold secret meetings, my brother Sin gathering them together and delighting them with his foolish thoughts and deliberations. Alas ! I was myself actually called upon to confirm the story of what we had heard in the imperial gardens. I was asked to say that the threatening roar came from a wild beast caught by cunning and powerful hunters and placed by them

in a great barred chamber, where he was
harmless.

Certainly I did not tire of explaining to
the hesitant that the dweller on the other
side of the river Mairure could not possibly
be in a cage, and that the roaring proceeding
from the cage was simply one of those
inexplicable phenomena which again and
again prove too much for weak human
reason, and about which it is better to
preserve silence. But they did not listen
to me, and were more ready to believe the
evil suggestion of my brother Sin.

At length there grew up a decided opposi-
tion of opinion—one half the people believ-
ing one way, one half the other. The one
half held to the tradition of our fathers
and preserved the belief that he who dwells
in the impenetrable thickets of the other
side of the stream is incomprehensible to
the human kind, and that he comes out of
the Jungle by night, announcing to the
villages by his roaring that he requires
another sacrifice. They held also that his
presence near a village brought good fortune,
saving us from many calamities and giving
us success in the hunt and at our labours.
The other half, with absurd vehemence and
obstinacy, repeated the foolish story of the

227

beast in the cage and turned a deaf ear to the wisdom of their elders.

There was much confusion and exasperation, fights, murders even, and brother rose against brother, son against father. Throughout all the country - side sweet peace was broken and quarrels began.

V

At last the wise Bellessis became possessed of a wily but deceptive thought, and many who liked to find middle paths were brought to a peaceful state of mind. Thus spake the wise Bellessis :

" Our fathers taught us to reverence the dweller in the woods who takes of us human sacrifice, and the teaching of our forefathers should in no wise be forgotten or laid aside. The whole system on which our life is framed would fall to pieces if we learned to have no fear before the eyes of green fire that shine on us out of the darkness of our nights. And if we elders and teachers should encourage a frivolous and neglectful attitude towards the mysterious one, it is certain that our boisterous and self - willed youths, dismissing the serious thought, losing the trembling in the night, will fall into the most excessive debauch and rascality."

The old men and the teachers welcomed these wise words with loud commendations, but having thus ingratiated himself in the heart of the elders the wise Bellessis went on and tried to make himself pleasing to the foolish. Thus he spake :

" On the other hand, we cannot doubt the probity of our common friend Melech, and the truth of the story his son tells. They say that they saw a finely ornamented place they call a cage, but which was no doubt a magnificent apartment worthy to be the palace of the dweller on the other side of the river Mairure. They heard a voice proceeding from this wonderful palace. It seemed to be the roaring which we know, and both Melech and Sin fell down in reverence to him who was in the cage. Then our rash Sin actually dared to look up and see what it was that roared thus at that time ; Melech and Sin were bowed to the ground, but the rabble in the garden laughed at them and gave a witness of their impoliteness. And Sin saw that that which roared was like a beast. Such is the story they brought home from the great city, and how can we disbelieve it ? And why cannot the dweller on the other side of the river Mairure have the appearance of a beast ? What does the devourer of our young ones demand of us ? Do we not know that he wants living flesh and blood ? We know he does not roast his meat or smoke it or salt it, but just devours it live. But how do we know that he needs flesh that is human ? If we build him as fine a place as that which was given the beast in the Emperor's menagerie, will he not bless our work ? Perhaps when we have built a palace for him he will change his desires and prefer to be fed with living calf or lamb."

The young men and the girls welcomed this speech with wild shouts and exclamations.

" Let us build a palace," said they.

The more foolish even dared to say, " Build him rather a cage and drive him into it. He has lived on our loveliest long enough." These were very stupid young ones truly, for they thought that life was the greatest blessing.

But in vain did the wise and aged strive to restrain the people in the faith of their forefathers ; in vain did they try and save them from the fearful act. Alack ! Even the aged, many of them, were won over to the young, for they loved their children more than they should.

VI

While they were building what they called a palace, but which was after all only a cage, several of the more impatient made a party and went to the other side of the river Mairure to hunt with arrows and spears. Of course they met their doom.

And another thing happened which greatly confused the honourable people of our countryside and emboldened the youth.

Young Zakkir, one of the bravest and cleverest of our hunters, went by himself and abode in the jungle a long time. We gave him up for dead ; and since he did not return the girls sang him sweet funeral chants.

But a week later Zakkir returned, weak from loss of blood, covered with horrible wounds, but all the same radiant with joy and daring. Very unwillingly and evasively did he answer the questions of the oldest of us, but we often saw him talking to his comrades and the young fellows in lonely places. Very soon a rumour was spread through the village that Zakkir had met the dweller on the other side of the river Mairure and had battle with him.

We could not tolerate the blasphemous stories and the enmity which was being worked up against the oldest and wisest of the village. So Zakkir was taken and put to the torture in order that we might know what had in truth befallen him.

But Zakkir did not endure much torment, he confessed, and we listened to him in dread. These were his words :

" The night was calm, and there was no moon when I approached the thicket that stretches a three days' journey beyond the river Mairure. My dagger was sharp and ready, my arrows poisoned, for I had firmly resolved to follow up and kill the monster. Suddenly, as near from me as a maiden stands looking at the youth she loves, as near as a little child throws a stone at the first attempt, I heard the roaring break forth. Moved by the power of the habit I fell down on my face on the earth and waited. I heard the heavy approach and the crackling of dry branches under feet. I waited. But a cold lizard slid along my leg as I lay and reminded me of the Emperor's menagerie and the story of the beast in the palace. I already felt his hot and fiery breath upon

me when I jumped to my feet and pulled
out my dagger. I don't know whether he
whom I saw was of the stock of demons or
of wild beasts, but he was immense fierce,
green-eyed. His jaws were open to devour
me, and the great white teeth made me
tremble. In truth, whether demon, god, or
beast, he is mighty and terrible. I don't
know how I kept my feet and did not fall
down again before him. It was some power
stronger than I that kept me face to face
with him and made me slave of fate. I
resolved to fight the monster whatever he
was. The beast crouched to spring like a
cat, and once more gave out the terrible
roaring which filled me with quaking. But
I followed his movements, and when he
sprang I turned craftily and hid behind a
tree. The beast prepared to spring again.
His failure seemed to give him a grieved
and shamed appearance ; he slunk away
and hid himself—cunning, cautious, evil.
I hurriedly prepared an arrow, and its
poisoned copper thrummed in the air and
struck the beast as he sprang a second time.
This time I did not succeed in dodging, and
the cruel claws rent my body. But I
plucked forth my dagger and fought with
that till I fell to the ground unconscious

from loss of blood. What happened I know not, but the beast went away without touching my body again. When I regained consciousness night was already over. As I lay, weak and smeared with blood, I saw the trace of the beast's footsteps away from me. Then I understood that I had wounded him grievously, and that he had gone away to die perhaps, perhaps to heal his wounds with forest leaves."

The old men deliberated a long while over the crime of Zakkir—could not make up their minds what to do, but at last the crafty Bellessis made a suggestion that won much praise.

"Let us wait till we hear the roaring again," said he. "If we hear the voice again that will show the victory of the dweller on the other side of the river Mairure over death, and we will then deliver to him Zakkir, naked and bound. So shall we be requited for the insult, and his anger not fall upon us."

The boys and girls of the village rejoiced, assuming that the beast was dead. "He is dead," they cried; "he will not come and roar any more outside our houses."

They crowned the rash and beautiful hunter with flowers, danced round him, and sang, and the sounds of flute and cymbal rose higher than the clouds.

But their joy did not last. Not a week passed before we heard the threatening voice once more.

And Zakkir was taken, made naked, bound, and placed in the jungle beyond the river. Next day, not far from the place where we left him, we found his bones. The boys and girls wept inconsolably, and the memory of Zakkir was ineffaceably printed on their hearts. But the elders cursed the daring one.

VII

But behold, the painted palace was ready. We placed it on the shore of the river Mairure, just at the place where he walks when awaiting his victim. In the cage we put for him as a last and dainty human victim the young and beautiful Hannai, taking away her dress so as not to put him to any unnecessary trouble.

We did not wait long. He came for his prey. We went to meet him with music and chanting. There was a strange excitement among all those who expected for the first time to see him face to face. And many felt a sweet pleasure at the thought that they would henceforth meet him openly with songs rather than as before in secret and with sorrow.

We were all attired as for a festival, our skins annointed with sweet oils, our heads crowned with flowers and sweet-smelling herbs. Not one of us carried a weapon—we obeyed the advice of the oldest, who warned us not to anger him with the sight of arms as one of us had already so foolishly done. Calmly and joyfully we went forth to meet him, singing the sacred hymns. Nearer and nearer sounded his voice, and behold at last the velvet light of our torches fell upon his face.

We stood around the cage, leaving him a wide and open road to the door of it. But he did not enter and take his victim, but bounded into a crowd of our children and struck to earth my daughter Lotta.

He tore the dear body of my daughter Lotta, growling with greediness, mewing with pleasure, and I looked up suddenly and I saw that he to whom we had for ever bowed ourselves, and for whom we had sacrificed an infinite number of our tribe, was indeed a ferocious bloodthirsty beast, strong only because we were weak, dreadful only because we trembled before him.

We also saw how the beast's body was yellow with ugly blotches of black upon it, and we cried out through our wailing, "Truly it is a wild and evil beast. Now we have seen with our eyes who it is that dwells in the thickets beyond the river Mairure, and we know the miserable fate of our children who have been victims, and of Zakkir, devoured by the ferocious, senseless beast."

But the beast set upon us again and took another victim. We fled, and he followed after us, tearing many with his claws, and choosing for his prey the youngest and sweetest.

On that day the beast was glutted with our blood. We shut ourselves in our huts and mourned. And we prepared to take vengeance.

VIII

The days went on. The crafty beast hid himself. There were diverse opinions held about him, but not many adhered to the ancient faith. Many rash youths perished in the jungle through incautious hunting.

The aged for the most part reproved the youths, saying, "Foolish ones, what do you strive for? What do you want? Think what will happen if you kill him? How

237

can we live without him ? You will over-throw all the traditions of our ancestors—but upon what will you rebuild our life ? "

Alack ! We did not know about that, nor did we care to think. All we wished was to be rid of the cruel beast !

And, behold, one morning there were joyful shouts ringing through the village streets, and all the children ran about crying, " The beast is wounded ! The beast is dying ! "

The girls of the village clapped their hands and danced and sang, saying, " The beast is dead, is dead ! "

On the banks of the river Mairure the beast lay dying, wounded by a poisoned arrow. His green eyes burned with power-less rage, and his fearful claws tore the earth and the herbage, all defiled by his foul blood.

Those who still feared the beast hid themselves in their huts and wept.

But we rejoiced that day.

We didn't think how we were going to live.

We did not consider who might come to the shore of the river Mairure and enslave us by another and more evil tyranny.

The Candles

THERE were two candles burning, and many lamps along the walls. A man was reading from an exercise-book, and others were silent and listened.

The flames trembled. The candles also listened — they liked listening; but there was a draught from somewhere, and they trembled.

The man finished. The candles were blown out and the people went away.

And it was just as before.

There was one grey candle burning. A woman sat and sewed. A child slept, and coughed in his sleep. There was a draught from the walls. The candles wept white, heavy tears. The tears trickled away and froze. It began to dawn. The woman with red eyes still sewed on. She blew out the candle. She sewed on.

And it was just as before.

Three yellow candles were burning. A man lay in a coffin—yellow and cold. Someone was reading from a book. A woman wept. The candles were dying from fear and sorrow. A crowd arrived. They sang; they flung incense. They lifted up the coffin. The candles were blown out. They went away.

And it was just as before.

FINIS